HOT SHOT

A MINNESOTA RAIDERS NOVEL

EDEN DUNN

HOT SHOT

When my sister told me she had hired a new nanny by the name of Esther to watch my rambunctious kids, I expected an elderly grandmother type.

I was completely wrong. *Utterly* wrong.

Esther Richardson might have been a child prodigy violin virtuoso in her youth, but right now she's making waffles like a master and completely showing me up in every way possible. She's also walking around in sexy outfits and making my life miserable.

As captain of the Minnesota Raiders professional hockey team, I'm all business. I'm Puck Daddy on the ice. At home, I'm trying to keep my hands off of Esther—and failing.

I haven't had feelings like these for a woman since my wife died. Esther is my kids' nanny. It's wrong to want her this badly. Isn't it? I no longer know.

One thing's for sure: I want out of the Single Dad Hockey Players Club. Can I convince Esther to give me a chance? To give us a chance to see where this goes?

Hot Shot is Book 1 in the Minnesota Raiders series

1

GRAY

Typical Sunday morning madness.

On the ice, I was the captain. I was in charge and I commanded respect. My team knew exactly how hard I expected them to work because I was beside them the entire time, putting in the same blood, sweat, and tears, maybe more.

I played center for the Minnesota Raiders professional hockey team and grown men feared me when they encountered me on the ice. In the locker room, what I said went. I had a reputation for being firm but fair and I earned every bit of the respect I received.

Yeah, but that was for my job on the ice.

The same could *not* be said for my home life, where my three children ran rings around me and pretty much got away with anything and everything. At home, apparently, I was Dad the Pushover. Dad, the one you could cajole with a grin or present a pouted bottom lip to and get your way. Dad, the one who tried my hardest and still nothing I did seemed to add up to the right total.

That hadn't always been the case. When my wife

Rachel was alive, this place ran like a well-oiled machine. Until the cancer stole that life from us. The cancer stripped her of everything except her beautiful golden heart before it took her away from me, from her family, irrevocably.

"Widower" is not a label you want when you're only in your late thirties.

And although I hated to admit it, even a few weeks ago things here ran more smoothly. That was until my sister Sophie decided to hook up with my teammate Lucky and moved out, leaving me alone with my three holy terrors for the first time since my wife died.

I could have pulled out my own hair. Not that I wasn't happy for Sophie. I definitely was, because she had never glowed the way she did around Lucky. For some reason, the man made her happy.

And it didn't pay to complain any more than I already had. Sophie had stepped in and helped me and my kids for the past three years when she didn't have to and I would be forever grateful for the way she put her life on hold for me.

She deserved her own life and family and future now. It would be unfair of me to hold her back and keep those things from her, especially when she seemed to have found someone—*gag*—who loved her back.

I still wasn't ready to forgive Lucky for making the moves on my baby sister. Huh, some best friend. Well, former best. I wasn't quite ready to give the title back to him yet.

Sophie did a lot for us, for which I would be *eternally* thankful. But it wasn't until she left that I realized how much. In this house, her absence was felt keenly and across the board. The kids didn't want to admit how badly but I had no problem crying myself to sleep at night wishing I'd done things differently with Sophie. Well, a little crying.

There was only so much you could do to keep good help outside of chaining her to the kitchen stove.

She'd left Candace, Georgia, Ryan, and me on our own. The days went on and turned into weeks. It became pretty clear to me I was in charge of nothing and no one respected dear old Dad. How had *that* happened?

Sophie and I had always had a good cop, bad cop thing going with the kids. Turned out you can't be both at once if no one knows what's going on, least of all the cop.

"Keep the noise down!" I called out, barely heard above the screaming.

No one paid me any mind. And I couldn't hear myself think.

Sunday morning, and a week to go before the start of hockey season. I needed help and I needed it ASAP. Enter Sophie to make up for the handicap she'd left me with.

I've got the perfect gal for you, big brother. Just you wait. You'll see.

Nope, no more waiting.

I was elbow-deep in pancake batter and according to my eldest, Candace, I didn't even know how to make a pancake properly. Why? Because Aunt Sophie made a smiling face of chocolate chips in their Sunday pancakes and I did not.

Pathetic.

Candace had given me a heartbreaking pout that tugged at my insides. Message received. I sucked.

"Daddy! The pancakes are lumpy and you forgot the chocolate chips," she told me again. Her blue eyes were wide and pained.

My wife's eyes.

"Next time I'll get it right, baby. Be patient with me." I leaned over and kissed the top of her head, trying to ignore the mess of knots and tangles I probably should have done something about days ago. She was eleven. Wasn't she old enough to do it herself?

Be grateful. I should take advantage of these times because once she hit those teen years head on, I knew I'd be public enemy number one.

Kisses would be the first things to go.

"Yeah, sure, Daddy. I'll remind you." Of course she would. Sharp as a tack and memory of an elephant, that one. Of all my kids, Candace was the most like her mom. She even looked like Rachel, with her flowing blond hair and a smattering of freckles across her nose. Candace was also the most athletic, and she actually loved attending my hockey games.

It made a father proud.

"Do you think the nanny will make us pancakes?" she asked slyly.

Ugh, the nanny. She'd be here soon. I wondered what she'd think about this whole set-up.

"Of course she will," I answered with an absent nod.

The new nanny, who was expected any minute now, would work hard for me. She would make my life easier and pick up where Sophie left off, if my little sister was to be believed. And cooking? Yup, part of the job description.

If my daughter wanted chocolate chip pancakes, then "Mrs. Doubtfire" could make them, whether she approved or not. Not that she'd be walking into a clean kitchen. Quite the opposite.

I groaned, leaning back away from the stove and trying to work out the crick in my neck.

My feelings about the nanny's arrival were mixed. The house looked like a bomb had gone off and my children were feral. There were meltdowns and mood swings now the likes of which we hadn't experienced since

Rachel died and made even worse since our family trip to Florida.

Talk about disaster.

The kids missed Sophie as well as their mom, even though my sister was now living just down the road. Still, it didn't seem close enough.

Okay, sure, some of the moodiness was a result of my poor culinary skills—too much sugar and fast food—and some just lack of routine. Or would it be disruption of routine? They'd gotten along fine until Sophie abandoned ship for her new boyfriend's place.

A nanny would surely help with those things. I had the hockey season starting soon and I just couldn't do all this alone.

When Esther Richardson arrived today, she would certainly have her work cut out for her, I thought with a chuckle as I flipped a pancake.

I'd allowed my sister to interview and hire a nanny because I trusted her judgment and she knew exactly what the job entailed. Working for me wouldn't be easy. My schedule was a bear during hockey season. My kids were unruly, and I had puck bunnies and autograph hunters and paparazzi and tabloid reporters chasing me whenever I left our gated community. It wasn't an easy role to fill but Esther was going to be *very* well compensated for her trouble. I'd make sure of that.

It would be different, for sure, having an older woman here, and having someone who wasn't family living with us full-time. My mother-in-law visited a few weeks a year but I found her presence stifling, even though I loved Gloria.

How would it be with a twenty-four hour a day live-in Gloria type? Without the legal ties?

Well, as Sophie pointed out, I just needed to *suck it up*.

I couldn't do this alone, which meant I had to accept help. Problem was I'd never been good at accepting help. It wasn't one of my strong suits.

"Daddy, I'm hungry!" Georgie called from the table, one front tooth missing and her little hands fisted around her knife and fork. She brought both down on the table with an echoing bang to emphasize her point. Brunette like me, like Sophie, and always lugging around a book or two. She was the monster who prodded everyone else into madness. A *cute* monster, I mentally corrected.

"I know, I know."

I plopped several non-smiling and non-chocolate-chip pancakes onto their plates, prepared to tell my kids to hush up and eat, when the doorbell rang. The rest of the failed food sat in a pile on the counter, steaming slightly.

"Okay, guys, dig in. I'll be right back," I declared, heading toward the front of the house.

The new nanny was here.

As soon as I stepped out of the kitchen, the kids started bickering. My eyes rolled back of their own accord. I didn't have time to deal with it right now. Hopefully, they'd start filling their mouths with pancakes and stop fighting before I got back with the nanny. I didn't want her seeing them at their worst right off the bat. It paid to make a good first impression.

Being a very successful and nicely paid NHL hockey player meant my house was huge. Too much for one guy to clean. Apparently Sophie had taken care of those little things too, I decided, walking through several rooms in total disarray as I made my way to the front door. She'd been blessed with a logical, organized mind and a firm hand. Those traits must have skipped me and gone straight to her.

Had she talked to the new nanny about cleaning duties,

too? Or would I have to retain my part-time housekeeper for that?

I caught sight of myself in the mirror in the foyer and stopped dead in my tracks. I had pancake batter on my cheek, a dishcloth over my shoulder. I looked a mess. I wasn't a bad-looking guy on a normal day. The chaos brought out the worst in me. My chestnut-colored hair was tousled, green eyes wide and slightly glazed.

Welcome to Sunday with the Wrights, Ms. Esther. Get ready for a baptism of fire, I thought as I pulled open the heavy oak door as the bell rang again. *Show time.*

Instead of the nanny, I opened the door to find a short young woman in a black t-shirt and a pair of dark jeans that hugged her curves. Her mouth was a perfect bow shape and her eyes wide and blue–green like a tropical ocean. I was at least a foot taller and towered over her, suddenly feeling like the Hulk.

My first thought? She was sexy as fuck and I had no idea who she was or how she made it past the security gates of our community and on to my doorstep. Maybe she had the wrong house. Disappointment gnawed. Or maybe I had a sexy new neighbor I hadn't known about. That could be fun.

Hope bloomed.

My eyebrows rose and something stirred to life in my shorts. I narrowly resisted slapping both hands over the area. The stranger watched me closely, the tail end of her raven-black braid dangling just below her breasts.

I felt like I'd just played a hard game on the ice and was breathless, knocked out, because I've never been as viscerally attracted to a woman in my life. Not even, I thought with a large dose of guilt, my late wife. My existence since Rachel hadn't been monastic by any means, but I hadn't exactly met a woman who made me feel quite this hot this quickly. Guilt grew and shifted and slammed into me—right along with lust.

"Who the hell are you?" I barked out the question and instantly regretted my tone. *It's not like it's her fault for being built like that.* Built like a goddess, like a—

"Aren't you expecting me?" the woman asked, her brow furrowing. Her cheeks flushed a delicate shade of pink as she stepped back to check the address. "Maybe I don't have the right house number."

"I'm expecting *someone*," I said, clutching the doorjamb. My words implied it wasn't *her*.

"826 Greenwich Place? Yep, I'm definitely in the right place. Hi there. I'm Esther." She cocked a thumb toward her chest.

Not helping, Esther, not helping. I didn't need her pointing at her truly excellent rack right now. I'd never seen a simple cotton t-shirt look so good on a woman.

Oh. Wait—

"*You're* Esther," I repeated slowly. *This has to be a mistake.*

"Who's Esther?" my son Ryan asked from behind me. I held him back before he could step outside and investigate.

I had been expecting an older woman, maybe a grandmotherly grey-haired widow or spinster. Certainly not this hot little bombshell. *This* I would never have agreed to.

The woman couldn't know why I was confused, or why I was holding my son inside the house. She reached out her hand, keen to salvage the situation since I was unable to.

"Let's start again," she said in a smooth, rich alto, "shall we? I'm Esther Richardson, your new nanny. You must be Gray Wright. It's very nice to meet you."

2

ESTHER

Grumpy Gray, as I'd christened him within the first few moments of meeting, took my extended hand, and his eyes shifted down to where our fingers touched, not happily. More reluctant than anything else.

I was too busy tuning in to the heat radiating up my arm and through my body to say any more to him. Then I felt it.

Boom, fireworks.

My eyes darted up to his.

Uh-oh. Fireworks were *bad*. Fireworks were inconvenient at the very least. He was my new boss. He was in a terrible mood. No fireworks allowed.

Who got fireworks from a simple handshake, anyway?

I hadn't even crossed the threshold to my new job yet so this had to be shut down and shut down quickly. I pulled my hand back and gave him a small smile.

"Hi," I said again to fill the silence. "Nice to meet you, Mr. Wright."

I'd made the connection that the man was some sort of athlete before I drove over, which explained the big house in the fancy gated neighborhood. His sister had acted like he was some big deal when she interviewed me.

I guess I should've paid more attention.

To be fair, the job had sounded reliable, the house was located in a great area, and the pay was fantastic. I had plans for that money, big plans, so I was thrilled when she offered me the gig. Just because I came from money didn't mean I had much of my own, outside of stocks and bonds and a trust fund. Not enough liquid assets for sure. I needed pocket change at the very least. Hence the nanny job.

Glancing behind Gray into the massive foyer filled with huge pieces of furniture and a lot of marble, I scowled. It wasn't fair but it really irked me that athletes were paid so much money. You'd never see an artist with a house like this. Heck, I was being paid more as a *nanny* for a rich athlete's kids than I had been paid by the symphony when I'd played with them.

It was ridiculous. But here I was.

Shaking my head, I returned my attention to the scowling, towering man in front of me. The same one who hadn't moved to let me into the house yet. Whatever his profession, he was clearly good at it, and I couldn't deny it had given him the body of a Greek god. His arms had muscles upon muscles, and the faded shirt he wore stretched across a hard, wide chest. I saw the perfection of his definition even beneath the fabric.

What? No, stop that!

I was really not one to ogle a man's muscles. Okay, not saying I was blind and I never looked when the occasion called for it, but I'd always been a brain-over-brawn kind of gal.

Gray Wright is not my type.

My type was nerdy and skinny and intellectual and...

well, *beta*, to be honest. This guy was so *not* those things. At. All. It was a pity my libido refused to accept the memo. Gray looked more like the alpha type of male to punch first and ask questions later.

He's not my type, he's not my type.

However, that did not seem to matter where my physical reaction to him was concerned. He was my new boss. I told my body to quash its demands. My lady parts were going to have to learn to ignore—or at least cope with—his hotness.

As well as being hot as hell, he was also adorably befuddled and confused. Maybe that was the part I liked. I glanced up into his handsome face, covered in a day or two of scruff, and took a closer look at him. His rich brown hair pointed every which way and he looked like the day had already worn him out and he'd like to go to bed.

The longer I stared, the more he seemed to collect himself. His next words were an apology I hadn't expected. "I'm sorry. It's madness here today, Ms. Richardson," he hurried to say.

"Esther."

"What?"

"Call me Esther, please."

He shook his head. "I'm not in my right mind. It's nice to meet you as well, um, Esther. And call me Gray. Everyone does."

"Not me," Ryan said. "I call him Dad."

"Um...well, come in. Do you have any bags to bring inside?"

He searched around my feet and then his eyes fell to the driveway where I'd parked. I saw him give my pink Mini the once-over. Maybe he was wondering how he would squeeze his enormous frame into my clown car.

I'd actually like to see that one day.

"I'll get them later," I said with a small laugh. My gaze landed on the batter splattered across his shirt. "Looks like you are in the middle of breakfast."

The comment seemed to bring him back to reality. "Something like that," he muttered. "Come on in."

I followed him inside a cavernous foyer with a sweeping staircase to the next floor and an echoing marble floor so shiny you could see your reflection in it.

"This is quite a house," I said, and instantly wished I'd thought of something more interesting. I didn't really know *what* to say. The house was a mansion. A bona fide mansion.

I grew up with money but our money was old money. It lent itself to a certain aesthetic, a certain décor style that verged on Early American. Gray's house? This thing was next level. If Gray made this kind of cash himself on the basis of his sports skills, then kudos to the man.

"And who are you?" I asked the small boy who suddenly came into full view after hiding behind his father. He had the same wild hair and smile as his dad.

Gray introduced me to Ryan, who immediately came over and took hold of my hand, dragging me through the house. Well, that was easy! He took to me instantly.

One kid won over, two to go.

We walked into the kind of kitchen I'd seen in lifestyle magazines, but with two girls sitting at the table bickering. They stopped, looked me up and down with wide eyes, and I saw their father in them both, though more in one than the other. A bit less so than I did in the little boy who had stuck to my side.

One girl must take after her mother. The other had a distinctive *Gray* look, the same as the boy.

When Sophie interviewed me, she'd given me the low-down on the kids. I knew all about the three of them. It was the way Sophie spoke about them, and her brother, with such love. It was what made me want to take this job.

I knew immediately without being told: I was needed here.

I hadn't been a nanny for terribly long. It was more of a side-step while I rethought my life path. Part of the attraction was to work with solid families where I would feel needed. Giving to others gave me a chance to figure out what I wanted for myself.

"This is Candace, my oldest at eleven. Then Georgia, who goes by Georgie, she's eight. And Ryan you met at the door. He's the baby of the family at five years old." Gray introduced the kids and they mumbled their welcomes. Ryan was still holding my hand.

"Please, keep enjoying your breakfast," I said, smiling at them, encouraging them to do the same. "I'm looking forward to getting to know you."

Beside me, Gray grumbled something under his breath that sounded like "I'm not sure anyone was enjoying themselves before you got here." I smothered a chuckle.

"I think they're doing well enough." Except I saw the pile of untouched pancakes still on the countertop and the smoke rising from the stove.

After offering me coffee, Gray told me to take a seat at the massive kitchen table. I did so and watched the kids, my hands wrapped around the warm mug. The girls gave me serious side-eye and pushed their food around their plates. I knew what they thought. I was an unwelcome intrusion in their lives and they made sure I was very aware of their opinion.

The little boy peppered me with tons of questions,

leaning forward like he couldn't wait to hear what I had to say. Did I have kids? Did I have pets? What was my favorite animal? My favorite superhero cartoon?

I saw immediately that he and I would be firm friends before the end of the day.

"Okay, enough," Gray told Ryan with a head shake. "You're overwhelming her."

Were the kids like this with everyone? He didn't seem too frustrated at the endless stream of chatter. Maybe it was normal.

"Ry, let's grab Esther's things and then we'll show her to her room. Girls, be nice while we get the bags. I don't want to hear you arguing again."

His voice held a warning I had no doubt these two had zero intention of heeding. They looked like they were plotting my demise right there at the kitchen table.

Meanwhile, Ryan raced after his father toward my car, the keys I'd handed him rattling as they went.

I stood next to the table while I waited. Candace turned toward me slowly and let her eyes wander up and down my small frame, clearly finding it lacking. Yeah, she wasn't thrilled with me at all.

Would I be able to change her mind? I hoped so.

"So you're our new nanny." She stabbed at her pancake and pointed the bite at me as she spoke. Her attempt to intimidate me was adorable. I kept my face emotionless to hide my amusement. "I don't need a nanny," she informed me.

Her sister nodded in agreement. "Me either. I'm eight. I'm a big girl."

"*You* probably do, 'cause you're only little," Candace replied grandly.

"Am not." Georgia poked her tongue out at her sister. "I'm *eight*. I am a big girl. *Ryan* is little."

"Well, ladies, thank you for letting me know how you feel." I always liked to encourage kids to share their thoughts and feelings. "I know your dad travels a bit for work, though, and because it's illegal for kids your age to stay alone, he probably just wants me around for that reason. And for Ryan. It's clear to me you are both responsible young ladies. Shall we check with him when he gets back?"

My comment was greeted with a narrowing of the eyes and a mumbled "Not right now" from Georgie.

Yeah, I didn't think so. I was pretty certain their dad had already given them plenty of information about how the whole non-related live-in nanny deal was going to work. They wanted to shake me down.

I was determined to be unshakeable.

Sophie had given me a pretty decent brief about what I'd face, but I knew it was going to be a little different compared to what Gray himself had in mind. We'd all figure it out as we went along. I was sure of it.

The girls continued to push the pieces of pancake around their plates and I wondered how Gray would react to me getting up and fixing them a proper breakfast. Clearly neither one was thrilled with what they currently had to eat.

As a child, I'd had a nanny or two when I was on tour and my parents refused to accompany me—or vice versa. I'd liked most of them well enough and a few of them I still kept in touch with.

There were going to be teething problems in any new situation. My own history put me in a unique position. I was able to see the current scenario from both sides. What my years on the road taught me was that an awesome care-giver was a beautiful thing. They became another presence in your corner and, if you were lucky, a solid person to lean on during tough times.

So, whether they wanted it or not, that's what I intended to be for these kids.

I saw the sadness in their faces. The sadness they wanted to hide even from their father and I wasn't sure he recognized the depths of.

Yes, an awesome caregiver was a beautiful thing.

Speaking of beautiful things, their grumpy dad chose that moment to return with my bags. Ryan wielded my violin case like a machine gun. I leaned down and grabbed it from him quickly. It didn't look important in its battered old case, but it was actually the only one of my belongings I truly treasured.

"Thanks, buddy, for bringing this in for me," I said, rescuing it from his grip without letting him know how worried I felt. Only once the case lay across my lap did I let out a sigh of relief.

"What's in there?" He scrunched his nose adorably as he asked.

And all four pairs of eyes turned to me, two brown sets, two green sets.

"A violin," I answered quietly.

"Oh. Do you play?" Gray asked. Surprise laced his voice.

I cocked my head at his tone. Did I...play? Wow, Sophie really hadn't told him anything about me, had she? The man hadn't even looked at my resume.

How odd. He must have really trusted her to make the right decision on his new hire.

It also explained why he'd had no idea who was on his

doorstep when he greeted me earlier. As he waited for my answer, he moved out the back door, pushing the sliding glass open to the patio.

I stood and followed. "I *do* play."

"*Nerd*," Candace whispered my way as I walked past her to follow Gray when he gestured.

"Yes, total nerd," I replied confidently. "And proud of it."

I was no hot-shot athlete. Until six months ago, I'd spent every waking hour of every day from the age of three *immersed* in the world of classical music. When I was her age I was so nerdy the other nerds felt cool beside me.

With a quick wink—one Candace *clearly* hated receiving—I followed the grumpy hot single dad and his cute son out the door, past a pool and toward a pool house that looked more like a small cottage. It had the same sloping lines as the house and an adorable little front patio section looking out on the kidney-shaped waters of the pool and the green space.

Behind, the rest of the yard stretched around the setup with just enough green for the kids to have room to run and play.

He paused on the deck while Ryan ran ahead to open the door. "The girls aren't too keen on having a nanny," he said at last, as though admitting to a grievous secret.

Oh, really? "I got that loud and clear."

Gray sighed. Well, it was half groan and half sigh. His hand went to his hair and messed up the strands further. "I'm sorry about their reaction. They're good kids but they don't like change and that's what this is for them. A huge change. They'd gotten used to having Sophie around."

I instinctively reached out and placed my hand on his forearm, and then immediately regretted it when his muscles tensed beneath my touch. *Okay, noted.* "It'll be fine, Gray," I answered. "I haven't even been here an hour yet. This is normal, it's like Nanny 101. It's expected that the first day the kids test you. Actually, the first week or two. So don't worry. Worry causes wrinkles."

He looked down at my hand on his arm until I removed my hand. Maybe it wouldn't be fine. I instantly took a step in the opposite direction.

His voice was gruff when he spoke. "I want this to work out, Esther."

"Me too," I replied earnestly, though I wasn't sure what it was I actually wanted right now.

What was it, again?

Oh yes, the job, the kids. Those were the things I was focusing on making work.

3

GRAY

Damn it all anyway.

One thing became abundantly clear the more time I spent around the woman: I needed to keep Esther as far away from me as possible. I knew it the moment I saw her standing at the front door and felt it every tense second she followed me through the halls on our house tour.

I spared a glance over my shoulder at the new nanny, her neck craned to take in the view of the backyard from the second floor.

My mind went down the long, slow slide into the gutter, landing on picturing her naked. Or sleeping. Or doing anything because she was literally the most beautiful woman I'd ever seen.

Outside of my late wife, of course. No one compared to Rachel.

I convinced myself that ogling my new nanny was just part of being human, because whenever I reacted to another woman I felt I was being unfaithful. Not, to be honest, that I'd ever reacted to another woman like I did to Esther.

She was beautiful in a completely different way, from her rich black hair to her ivory skin and her stunning smile. She held herself with natural poise and grace and took even the insanity of the house in stride.

Took *me* in stride when I'd stared at her like a confused and somewhat snarky idiot. I'd never forgive myself for the terrible first impression. I wasn't always suave but I was usually coherent.

She hadn't jumped when I snapped. I liked that. I was a big guy who was sometimes a bit of a grouch. It took a while for some people to warm up to me based on my appearance, and if she was going to be living here, working here, I'd need someone with a spine. A backbone. Someone who wasn't easily intimidated. She'd need that to deal with the three hellions that sprang from my loins, in addition to everything else.

And yet I was in no way prepared for Esther herself, for anything about her, and I was going to need some time to adjust to the reality of this sexy woman living here instead of the little old lady I'd been expecting.

Mrs. Doubtfire? Nope. Instead, the universe had gifted me a young Audrey Hepburn with curves. Didn't people say the universe sometimes had a perverse sense of humor? Now I believed it.

"Like I was saying, there's space on the second floor if you want. But I get the feeling you'd be more comfortable out in the pool house. It will give you a little more privacy."

"There's enough space in the house to have privacy," Esther replied. "Except you're right. I think the pool house is a good bet for right now."

"You'd think there's plenty of room here but apparently three floors are not enough," I responded with a grumble. "Everyone is always right on top of one another."

Really, who named their kid *Esther* these days, anyway? It was a relic of a name and definitely didn't fit the woman I couldn't stop staring at. Drooling at.

Get a grip on yourself, Gray.

This wasn't like me. I didn't lose my cool *ever*. Well, hardly ever—maybe occasionally on the ice. But least of all over a good-looking woman. I felt like I was back to age fifteen with a crush on my next-door neighbor, doing all I could to impress her while she never gave me the time of day.

"It's pretty much whatever you want," I finished lamely.

It sounded more like defeat than the open invitation I'd hoped for.

Ryan trailed us through the rest of the house, from the basement play space—a kid's paradise and an adult's apocalyptic nightmare—to the messy rooms on the second floor I'd been begging them to clean. Ryan added his own input to the tour. The kid certainly did want to make her feel welcome. One out of three was a start, at least.

We'd made our way back to the pool house after the tour. I pushed open the sliding glass door I probably should have cleaned before her arrival. Hell, I'd been thinking she'd stay on the first floor of the house to better accommodate arthritic hips.

Now I knew better.

And those hips...

Nope, time to focus.

I wanted to slap myself. This was the kind of shit that happened when one made assumptions. And when one let one's sister handle the arrangements instead of looking over the details oneself.

Message received. In the future, I'd have a firmer hand and take a keener interest when it came to hiring help. I'd scour the resumes and insist on a photo for every applicant, to avoid mistakes like this.

Still, she was a beautiful mistake.

"This place will definitely give you some privacy. It doesn't have its own kitchen but it's got a sink and a mini fridge, a decent-sized bedroom and bathroom, plus a little area you could use for..." For what? What did the woman like to do? Play the violin? "...anything you want. Anyway, the job isn't 24/7 unless I'm away for games. Then you can sleep in the house with the kids in one of the guest rooms. There are plenty of bedrooms available for you to choose from. If you want. I mean—" Wow, *think* much? "It might be better to have an adult on hand to watch them," I struggled to finish. "I'd feel more comfortable."

I'd certainly feel more comfortable if she'd stop looking at me with those eyes.

Esther shrugged. "Whatever works. It's entirely up to you and what is best for your lifestyle. I'm here to make things easier for you, Mr. Wright."

"Gray," I answered automatically.

Her smile stayed exactly the same. "Okay, Gray."

Odd how she hadn't mentioned hockey at all. Not my status, not the games, nothing. Definitely not the money or fame. Normally those were the first questions out of people's mouths.

She was looking around the bedroom at the queen-size bed and the small sofa in the attached side room with a less than critical eye instead of looking at me. Exactly as I'd wanted, except...when she did look at me? It was like she had no idea who I was.

Curious.

"Great." I rubbed my hands together. "So this space works for you?"

"Of course. It's nice and bright, very open. I appreciate your thoughtfulness in giving me options."

Thoughtful? Me? I was barely holding it together. "Yeah, sure."

I gestured for her to follow me and we made our way around the pool and back toward the house. In a few weeks, I'd have to break the pool cover out and put the chlorinated water I loved to bed for the colder months. Winter in Minnesota was no joke, and truly, I would have adored having something indoors so I could use the water all year 'round.

One of these days, once I cleared a few things off of my plate, I'd get around to it.

"You're free to use whatever facilities are here, too. The pool of course, and there's an infrared sauna in the basement, along with my gym. As long as it doesn't take away from watching the children. We can sit down with the kids in a bit."

"The house is certainly a lot more spacious than I'm used to at the moment." She wasn't cowed by the size or any of the amenities. "I grew up in a place of similar size, but since I moved out, it's just been me and my tiny apartment. Not even enough space for me to feel comfortable bringing a cat in. I've gotten used to it."

She tossed her braid over her shoulder and the movement captured me.

My son appeared out of nowhere with the stealth of the Unabomber. And damn if I didn't recognize the expression on his face. He'd gone so quiet, maybe I'd just forgotten he was there. "You have your own apartment?"

Esther offered Ryan a sweet and easy grin as she crouched down to his eye level. "I do! It's a cute little place with lots of plants and lots of light. I have a space for my violin and no neighbors, which is good because I'm sure they wouldn't want to hear me sawing away on the strings night and day. I'm on the top floor of a house and the other floors aren't even rented right now."

She was so kind to him. From the smitten way Ryan stared at her, I saw he already had a crush on her. Smart kid. I didn't blame him. I felt similar stirrings in myself.

Except I was a grown-ass man and a childish crush had no place in my life. I had obligations, a team to lead, and offspring to mold into productive members of society. Romance? Off the table. I'd gotten lucky once by meeting Rachel. People didn't generally get lucky twice in their lives.

I shoved my hands into my pockets. "Okay, come on. Let's get this over with."

On the way inside, I heard voices coming from the kitchen and although my first thought was suspicion, I recognized them all soon enough.

Eye roll time. Jesus, was there never a moment of peace around here?

When had my place become the neighborhood playground?

My sister Sophie and her—*ugh*—boyfriend Lucky were there, as well as my teammates Dominik and Alexi and their kids. The Single Father Hockey Players Club, I thought ruefully, had let themselves in without knocking.

Typical.

And don't get me wrong, I liked Lucky as a player and my once upon a time best friend. He was a good guy. I just had a lot of mental hurdles to get over knowing he and my sister were an item and were—*ugh* again—sleeping together. In the same bed. The back-stabbing move had taken me more than a little by surprise.

How long had I tried to prevent that exact scenario? Years. If I'd been a little more successful, Sophie would still be my nanny and I wouldn't be fighting my urge to strip Esther naked because Esther wouldn't even be here.

Stupid me for taking a vacation to Florida and leaving Sophie alone, unsupervised.

I scowled across the room when I couldn't hear my own thoughts over the din. Bless Esther's probably sexy heart, if the rest of her was anything to go by: she was taking the noise and chaos like a true professional.

She stood in the doorway to the kitchen with her hands clasped in front of her and the same sweet smile on her face.

Did it ever crack, I wondered? Or had she worked hard to be able to keep it in place?

"I didn't know I was hosting a party," I said with a deep grumble. It didn't seem to matter that I had not extended an invitation to my teammates. They gathered whenever they felt like it and made themselves at home. In *my* home.

My teammates laughed. "We're all here to meet the lovely Esther! You can't blame us, can you, Gray? Look at her." Dominik pushed away from the counter with his hand outstretched. With wavy dark hair, light eyes, and a killer smile, he was the team jokester and one hell of a goalie. "It's an absolute pleasure. I'm Dominik. Dom if you're nasty. I'm the star player of the Minnesota Raiders."

He took her hand in his and raised it to his mouth. I wanted to punch something. Anything. Or someone. Lucky was closest. He'd do nicely.

And Dominik was a shameless flirt. Sooner or later, I'd need to tell him that the woman was off limits. Off. Limits. She was my nanny, which meant Dom would have to behave in her presence or else.

My three children were running around the kitchen

island like godless heathens, Alexi's two right behind them, and Dom's son Erik sitting at the kitchen table eating the rest of the pancakes no one else had touched.

At least someone liked them.

On a normal day I was used to the bedlam. I was used to the hubbub and the madness because I had no choice. Today it rubbed me like sandpaper on my private parts. I wanted to tell everyone to get the hell out and leave me alone with Esther to get to know her better. Or maybe I should leave them all to the mess and find someplace to hide.

Recuperate, I clarified.

With Esther and the kids distracted by the company, I took the opportunity to pull Sophie aside. We crossed into the dining room and I closed the door behind us to block out at least a little of the noise.

"What did you do?" I barked out immediately.

She blinked up at me with soft green eyes, the same color as mine. She looked good, I begrudgingly admitted. She looked happy. "What? I hired you a great nanny. You should be down on your knees thanking me," Sophie said with her hands on her hips. "Well? I'm waiting."

Were my eyes rolled back in my head yet? Surely they could go a little farther. "You should have warned me. I was expecting a little old lady."

Sophie cracked up. "Your kids would *destroy* a little old lady. Are you kidding me right now? Get a grip on yourself."

Hmm. Well, she made a good point. "Did you have to pick someone so hot?" I griped.

"Ooh. You think she's hot? Wow, you're *not* actually dead," she quipped. "Good to know, big brother."

Nope, I thought, watching Sophie exit the conversation. I wasn't actually dead. But living with the new nanny may just do the trick.

4

ESTHER

Wow. Wow, wow, *wow*! These guys were all huge! I mean, these were four beefy single dads who apparently played hockey together. Or they were on the same team. Or something. I still wasn't up on the whole hockey thing. I'd have to educate myself as we went forward so I didn't sound like a complete idiot and embarrass Gray in public. And I guess Lucky was technically off the market as he and Sophie were an item.

Looking at the men together was enough to make a girl go a little mad from the sexy, *sexy* testosterone of it all. They definitely sucked the rest of the air from the room with their presence.

What would happen when the entire team converged? Were they all this stacked or were some of them a little more normal?

No wonder hockey had such a large fan base.

It was also a good thing Sophie had warned me going into this. She hadn't exactly prepared me for the full force of seeing them together in one relatively small kitchen.

She'd just said Gray hung out with a lot of guys from the team. But I knew enough to be forewarned.

And forewarned is forearmed.

"They're a lot to take in at once," she'd told me. "Too beefy for their own good. Well, except for my brother."

Actually, I thought her brother was the best-looking of the bunch, sorry to say.

Gray's kids, with the arrival of their friends, seemed to have chucked off whatever semblance of order they'd adopted when I first came and went full-tilt to the wall. They were no longer focused on feeling me out. Fine.

I leaned against the countertop with my arms crossed over my chest, taking stock. To be observant was the best weapon in my arsenal.

So far, this was what I knew:

Dominik was big and strong and handsome. The flirt, and the fun one. He wanted everyone to know that even though he was a single dad, he hadn't lost his spark, his fire. He cracked jokes at every opportunity, or whenever the energy seesawed to skew one way or another. A defense mechanism? I'd see soon enough.

Until this point, Alexi hadn't smiled. Not once. He stood at the edge of the pack, watching, and stepping in when it was warranted when the kids got a little too rough with each other. His little guy kept falling on his butt, trying to keep up with the big kids, and Alexi was always standing by to set him back on his feet. Good-looking and stoic, the one who stepped in at the last minute before things got too out of hand. He'd be the tough one to crack. He'd be the one to watch out for. He had visible tattoos on both arms and a scar across his left eyebrow. Definite bad boy vibes.

As for Lucky and Sophie, they were clearly newly in love. Still enjoying the cozy honeymoon phase of their relationship. Seeing love so fresh, through their eyes, was beautiful. Lucky must consider himself a charmer with his swarthy good looks. It was easy to see from the effortless way he took my hand, thumb brushing against my palm in a move he must have done so many times it was now second nature.

I watched Sophie and Gray peel off out of the corner of my vision for a little family conversation alone. Not sure what that was about but I'd find out about it soon if I was the subject matter. Or maybe I wouldn't.

"The kids are really comfortable with each other," I said to Dom when he slid closer to me. "It's good to see."

He was close enough that the merest shift would have our shoulders pressing together. Okay, down the line we might need to have a little chat about personal boundaries. I didn't appreciate people getting too far into my space. I'd grown up as an only child with distant parents. I wasn't used to this kind of thing.

"Yeah, they're great friends," Dom said. "It helps living in the same neighborhood. We kind of all made the decision to keep the kids close to each other location-wise."

"You chose the neighborhood together?"

"Well, sure," he answered. "The Single Dad Hockey Players Club needs to stay on the same page. In the rink and out."

"The rink... Now, do you play on artificial turf? Or is it real grass?" I asked. Maybe it was wood. Didn't one roller skate in a rink? I didn't know; I'd never been roller skating in my life. Richardsons didn't do those sorts of activities.

Dominik stared at me and blinked. Blinked some more and heat rose into my cheeks. Had I said something wrong?

"You...are sweet," he said at last, though he sounded choked. "Absolutely sweet."

"Why?" I asked with a laugh.

"Have you ever watched a hockey game in your life, Es?"

I wondered at the easy nickname. "I can't say I have, Dom."

Dom if you're nasty. My cheeks heated further. I wasn't nasty.

The kids were still running around and screeching like banshees. Boundless energy. They interacted with each other easily. They had clearly been friends for a long time, long enough for them to learn to work with each other, to group together with the typical pack mentality I knew belonged to children and canines.

"It's not football, it's *hockey.*" Dominik stressed the word. "We're the Minnesota Raiders. Do you really think we play on grass?" He waited for me to put things together.

Gray and Sophie rejoined the madness moments later and I glanced over at the pair. Not exactly a plea for help but perhaps close enough for them to see I needed to be rescued.

Well, not needed, but I'd appreciate one of them stepping in to save me from this embarrassment I'd brought on myself.

"Gray, hey, come here." Dom beckoned with his hand and barely controlled his laughter. "Did you know? Esther knows nothing about the NHL. Fancy that."

And then Gray was staring at me. His eyes bored through me in a way that wasn't exactly uncomfortable but certainly came close to making me squirm. "I didn't realize it was a prerequisite for this job," I answered smoothly.

I didn't even know what NHL stood for.

"Dude, she *literally* just asked me if we played on real grass or artificial."

Was it my imagination or had the rest of the room gone a bit quieter? Were there more eyes on me now than there had been before?

I should have done some research on the team before I came here. I knew better now and I'd never make the same mistake again.

Gray glanced over at his sister, who did nothing but shrug. Oh, she was enjoying this, I could tell. "Puck Daddy, there's no way I'd hire you a puck bunny as a nanny. I mean, come on. I have a reason for everything I do," Sophie said.

A puck bunny? "What's a puck bunny?" I was probably shooting myself in the foot for asking.

Dominik leaned closer to me yet again to explain, his breath tickling my hair. "A puck bunny is a woman who chases after the players with one particular prize in mind. Someone who speaks the lingo. Some puck bunnies follow certain teams through all of their games. Talk about an ego boost."

I thought about the same phenomenon happening with orchestras, too. It was probably much rarer than the puck bunny thing, but it wasn't unheard of. What would one call *those* women?

My mind immediately turned to my ex, the first chair viola for the Minnesota Philharmonic Orchestra. Everywhere we went, women flocked. Hounding him. Hitting blatantly and openly on him. Once when the two of us were standing together waiting for our transportation after a concert, one went so far as to physically shove me out of the way simply to get closer to him, resulting in an awkward fall for me and a couple of weeks of intense anxiety until it could be concluded that my sprained wrist had not suffered permanent—or career-ending—damage. And when he left me for someone else right after that, I realized he wasn't interested in anything permanent. At least with me.

My stomach roiled. I ignored it.

"Are these puck bunnies usually a problem for you?" I asked Dom.

How did Gray and the others deal with the attention? The same way my ex had?

Dom tipped back his head and laughed loudly, obnoxiously. "Honey, *never*."

Well, they were all single men. Single dads who deserved love. I'm sure they adored having the bunnies around to boost their egos. Except Lucky. He'd taken himself out of the equation.

"Esther?"

I glanced up at my name, my gaze falling on Gray as he crooked a finger for me to follow him. Guess it was my turn for a little dining room chat.

I shifted away from the din of the kitchen.

"Are you serious?" he began at once. He stared at me with his arms crossed over his chest. Not bothering to hide the drying flakes of the pancake batter still on his shirt. "You don't know a thing about the NHL?"

Oh. This was what he wanted to talk to me about? Not another deep dive into my references? "No, I don't. Is it a problem?" If so, I wanted to know now.

The wide grin he shot me told me everything. My lack of knowledge was in no way an issue for him. If anything, he looked relieved.

"Of course, I'm open to learning more about what you do as a profession," I offered, my hands wide in front of me. "If it makes my time with the children go a little smoother then I'll learn everything I can about what you do. After all,

I assume they are big fans of the Raiders? It might help me to be able to talk to them in the future."

Gray simply shook his head. "What you know or don't know about hockey is pretty irrelevant to me. But I appreciate..." He trailed off without finishing his sentence.

I didn't get a chance to hear anything else. The door to the dining room burst open and the youngest boys raced inside, trailed by Ryan swinging a paper towel holder as a sword.

There were no sacred spaces here, especially not when the gang was all gathered together. They were there for an impromptu barbecue, Sophie informed me moments later when I walked back into the kitchen. They were all staying for the food and the fun.

And from the way she spoke, these types of gatherings, this level of noise, was normal. Cookouts were the usual, and the week was considered strange and *un*usual without at least one.

Part of me didn't understand how one could have a get-together of this size without any planning whatsoever. The types of soirees I was used to would have taken at least a few days of preparation if not a week or more to get the details exactly right. People didn't simply *show up* and expect to be entertained and fed.

And rambunctious children making such noise simply wasn't tolerated. Children were expected to mind their nanny and entertain themselves, period. *Be seen and not heard, unless you're playing your violin;* that was pretty much the mantra of my own childhood.

I'd have to get used to the energy of this place. At home, where it was only me and my instrument, it was easy to forget how life marched on outside of those four walls. I'd wanted it that way, loved the peace and quiet. Or maybe I'd needed the reprieve from everything I went through leaving the orchestra behind. Leaving *him* behind.

For the rest of the afternoon, I sat apart and watched the kids. Ryan, bless his heart, shadowed me wherever I went. He was certainly a little sweetheart.

"This is totally cool," Sophie told me on the patio later. The sun began to set below the lines of the neighboring houses and the two of us were getting cozy.

"What is?" I asked.

She leaned her head over the back of the chair, her ponytail dangling behind her. Her eyes were closed and she looked wholly relaxed. "The impromptu cookouts. I mean, Gray's place has always been considered the hangout spot for the kids. They know they can come here and run off their energy. The big boys go to Dom's house when they need adult time away. There's a weekly poker night when they all like to play poker, lose money, drink too much, and generally make asses out of themselves."

Sophie took a sip of her lemonade, swallowing quickly when Lucky walked over to hand off his daughter, Natalie, to her. She began to bounce the baby on her knee.

"Will you mind the baby for a minute, baby?" he asked her. "Alexi wants to show us a new routine he's put into his workout. We're heading to the basement."

"Sure thing."

They paused for a sweet peck on the lips before Lucky walked off with the other dads.

"A poker night," I repeated softly, trying my hardest not to watch Gray's butt. "Interesting."

"Like I said, you'll get used to the way things work around here. Maybe you'll even be able to make better sense of it than I did." Sophie bounced the child on her knee some more until the little girl began to giggle.

Another interesting thing: Lucky's daughter boasted one green eye and one blue eye, exactly like her daddy. Natalie seemed very taken with Sophie, too.

"Thank you again for recommending me for this position," I said to Sophie. "I've never had the type of experience that involves cookouts and poker nights. I'm excited to see how things work out."

Gray, I'd noticed through the course of the afternoon, much preferred to engross himself in work talk with his teammates instead of chatting with me. He had also seemed to avoid eye contact.

Part of me bristled. What had I done to earn that kind of disinterest? Almost like he preferred to look anywhere else except at me. I'd stayed to the side to get used to the situation but he clearly hadn't felt inclined to help me.

Oh well. Things were bound to take a little getting used to, for everybody.

"It's going to work out," Sophie insisted. "I am sorry about Gray."

I almost choked on my lemonade. "What about Gray?"

"He can be a moody pain in the ass."

I crossed my legs, took another small sip of the lemonade Ryan had fetched for me. The girls, though...they were still aloof like their dad. It was only day one, I reminded myself. It was nothing new. After I'd left the Milwaukee Symphony, I'd spent the next six months on a remote movie set as the nanny for a spoiled child star.

Talk about moody!

I knew moody. I knew aloof.

And I knew *exactly* how to handle both.

5

GRAY

We made it to Wednesday and Esther hadn't run screaming from the house.

Yet.

In fact, I'd go so far as to say things were going along pretty well. The new normal wasn't perfect by any means but it felt like we were getting there. Until now, I'd managed to keep my hands to myself and I'd done what I considered to be an excellent job of not staring lecherously at the new nanny every chance I got.

Score one for Gray Wright. Someone needed to hand me a prize for my self-control.

I'd passed her earlier in the morning wearing a pair of denim shorts and a short-sleeved pink button-down shirt and I almost stumbled down the stairs and bashed my nose into the banister. Somehow the basic outfit hugged every delicious curve of the woman's body.

I wondered how it was that even in relatively modest clothing Esther still managed to look hot, but she did. Dammit, she did.

I stared at the ceiling as though I'd somehow receive an

answer. None was forthcoming. My terrible reaction was why I'd hauled myself down into the basement gym to work off my pent-up lust on the treadmill before the guys came over for weight training.

What else was a man to do?

Conversely, she seemed completely unaffected by me. That was good, very good. And bad because a big part of me *wanted* her to want me. I had feelings like everyone else. As I paused the treadmill, I reminded myself: Esther wasn't like the women I'd met over the past few years.

She wasn't going to fall at my feet because I was a big shot hockey player. In fact, if I had to hazard a guess, I'd bet my career had the opposite effect on this particular woman.

I heard my family moving around upstairs like a herd of buffalo. The girls would surely be giving Esther a semi-hard time with getting ready for school. Both of them. Candace in particular tried her damnedest to not like her new caregiver. Maybe she and I could bond over that.

Probably not the best parenting idea ever, as I was trying my damnedest not to think about Esther as well.

I knew Candace, in part, thought she was too old for a nanny, even though she was only eleven. The other part? Liking Esther might make her disloyal to her mother's memory. When Sophie had been here, things felt different. Sophie was family. Liking family didn't take anything away from the mother we all lost.

That was the part we had in common. My attraction to Esther made me feel like I was cheating on my wife, although Rachel had been gone several years and I hadn't even touched the new woman. Except Esther was the first woman I'd spent any real time with since Rachel and actually wanted to learn more about.

My sister didn't count.

Of course, moments after meeting Esther, the guys on the team had been smitten and had been ragging on me the last couple of days about my *hot new nanny*. Dominik found it especially amusing because that was the kind of guy he was.

And when they came over again today, they had no issue continuing the conversation.

"I am not going to bang the nanny, Dom, as you so delightfully put it," I told him during our training. He was lifting and I was spotting for him. "She's one hundred percent off limits. The woman lives in my home and works for me. You have to understand there are rules about this kind of thing."

I needed him to understand because I wouldn't always be around to intervene and put my foot down. The sooner Dominik learned to stay away from Esther, the better.

"She doesn't work for *me*," Dom replied, exactly like I knew he would. Partly it was just to rile me up, but I wasn't completely certain he wouldn't ask Esther on a date if I green-lighted the idea.

Actually I hated the thought of the two of them together. What did I have to say to make Dom understand? There were lines not to be crossed and Esther was one of them. "No, but she's off limits to you too, because we both know you'll mess this up for me."

Dom shrugged, his shorts tight on his frame as he continued his set of squats with bicep curls. Shirtless, as he so often liked to work out. "She might be up for just a casual little—"

"Off. *Limits*." I literally growled in his face, which just made him laugh.

He understood a little better than I did, at this point,

how deeply I'd gotten attached to my nanny. Did he even care? I wasn't sure.

"You won't last a week, Gray," he said before finishing his set and walking his half-naked ass toward the shower. "Mark my words!"

My buddy Alexi knew me better yet. His wife had died in an unfortunate car accident and he didn't really date either. His marriage had already been rocky and on the verge of collapse, but the man who had never been a ray of sunshine before now boasted he had an epic case of survivor's guilt.

Alexi watched our interaction quietly before offering his own brand of wisdom through a set of triceps kick-backs.

"I hope you take your own advice," Alexi warned me. His brows drew together in a harsh line. "You need to get out there again and date but not with someone who works for you."

"I know. It's just...she's the first woman I've really wanted," I admitted. "Still, I am going to keep it professional."

"You dated Mira for a few months."

I shook my head. "It wasn't the same with Mira."

How did I make anyone understand? This kind of attraction wasn't only rare for me. It was rare in *general*. The kind of instant chemistry one shouldn't—couldn't—take for granted.

Mira was a nice woman, and sure, we'd had our fun. We even hung out on occasion. But the draw simply hadn't been there for me to pursue it further. Mira had certainly never been around my kids.

Alexi gave me the evil eye for my comment and I knew what he was thinking. I *did* sound like a spoiled brat. The nanny was there for my children and I could not muck this situation up. We didn't need a revolving door of nannies in my house because I couldn't keep it in my pants.

"Which is exactly why you need to get out. Maybe someone else will light the spark and the problem will be solved. You still talk to Mira. Maybe give her another go. Or find someone else. Just not this one."

Alexi was probably right, I decided as I finished my workout and headed up to breakfast. Someone else might help take the pressure off of Esther. And Mira and I still talked, we still went out to dinner. She was a lovely lady.

She simply wasn't *my* lady.

The boys would leave the basement whenever they finished their routines. I wasn't worried about them, and I definitely wasn't about to offer them food. They'd stay forever if I started feeding them breakfast too.

"Let yourselves out when you're done," I called.

"Daddy! It's Waffle Wednesday," Ryan told me excitedly as I walked into the kitchen. He was swiping his waffle through a river of syrup and looked completely delighted with himself.

I didn't blame him. It was waffles. What's not to love?

Yesterday was Taco Tuesday and the day before was Meat-free Monday. Waffle Wednesday was something of a treat.

The girls slid off their stools when I turned the corner and raced upstairs to get their bags for school. Okay, had I done something to cause the mass exodus? "Well, good morning to you, too," I muttered after them.

I took a step toward Esther, who smiled up at me from behind the waffle maker. She was always looking up at me unless I was seated, such was our height difference.

I found I liked it a lot.

"I prefer Waffle Wednesday to Meat-free Monday, you should know," I told her in a low voice.

"You ate a whole steak for lunch that day, so hardly meat-free," she whispered back so my son wouldn't hear. He hadn't exactly been a fan of a meat-free day either. "Don't tell the kids."

"I need protein," I protested in return.

There was something intimate about whispering with an adult in my own home. It made me feel naughty and I kind of liked it, maybe a little too much. Rachel and I had had the same kind of humor. She'd always been laughing at something and forcing me to join her, the sound infectious. Things weren't quite so comfortable with Esther yet, but this was a good start.

"And protein you shall have. I figured you would want something a little heartier than just waffles to start your day. This is for you." She handed me a platter with bacon, sausage, eggs, and waffles, and our fingers brushed when I reached for it.

Like trying to grab the flame on a lit candle. I jumped out of the way before I burned myself on her.

"Yeah, thanks." I sounded gruff and ungrateful, which I hated.

Ryan finished his waffle and leaped up to get ready for school...leaving me alone with my sexy, still smiling nanny.

Way too alone.

I briefly imagined pouring syrup down the hint of cleavage Esther's top revealed and then licking it off of her. Slowly.

We needed some neutral topic, ASAP. "Tell me, exactly how many games of hockey have you seen?" I asked her. I used my fork to shovel a giant mouthful of eggs into my mouth.

"Live or on TV?" she clarified, counting her fingers for a second before forming a zero. "None."

Wow. *None.* I liked the sass but I had to ask, "Then why did you take this job? Tell me the truth."

I was rewarded with a throaty laugh for my comment. "The ego on you! You seriously think I'd be here to get close to the great hockey player Gray Wright? No offense but I don't know that you're even any good. I took the job because I'm a nanny and a good one and that's what your kids need. Doesn't matter to me if you're a lawyer or a marine biologist or a barista."

Oh.

She was right, of course. I did sound like an arrogant prick, but, well, welcome to my world. Women fell at my feet—men too, sometimes.

Because even if she didn't know it, *Gray Wright* had the stats to back up his ego. 1,500 points scored in my career so far, over 1,000 assists, and less than 500 penalty minutes.

In my world, Esther was the unusual one. Part of me found it hard to believe she knew nothing about hockey. Not even the vaguest idea. It was impossible for me to imagine life without hockey in it.

"Sorry," I said with a laugh. "It's just that everywhere I go, people want a piece of me and in turn a piece of my kids. I guess I'm kind of neurotic. You might be a secret stalker trying to auction my underwear online for all I know."

Esther shot me a dismissive look and wave of her hand and I couldn't help but notice her long delicate fingers. Yes, those were artist's fingers. "Don't worry about me. I'm only here to do my job. Your underwear is safe."

"Your job will inevitably include accompanying my kids to games sometimes."

I sliced off a bite of waffle, lifting it to my mouth, eyes closed.

God, the waffles were good. Even without Ryan's excessive amount of syrup the taste was out of this world. What kind of magic had Esther worked with the waffle maker?

When had I *bought* a waffle maker?

"They don't go to every game but they certainly take in their fair share. Candace especially loves the sport. You may learn to love it, too," I continued. "You'll also get to see what I'm talking about."

That earned me a firm head shake. "I think it's highly unlikely I'll grow into a diehard superfan. I'm not into any sports." She placed the dirty dishes in the sink. "Although it will, as you say, give me some insight into your work life, which could probably be helpful for dealing with the kids."

Wow, that sounded like a challenge to me—to find out what she *was* into and to get her into hockey.

Hmm. I wasn't supposed to care what my nanny was into to this extent. This was a problem.

"Are you driving the kids to school today?" I asked at last. "Or I can drop them off on my way to practice."

"You choose. Although I have to say, the school bus would be a better choice. Candace says they don't ride the bus." Esther shook her head. "I don't understand why." She shrugged. "You're the dad. What do you want to do?

What I wanted to *do* was *her*. But I had a feeling if I said that out loud, she'd have something bad to say about the sentiment. Seeing as how *doing her* wasn't an option, I'd just eat my delicious breakfast and drive my own kids to school.

I smiled over the last bite of waffle.

It wasn't all bad.

6

ESTHER

So far, I felt like things were going pretty well here in my new role.

The girls were very slow to warm up, with Georgie following her older sister's lead in keeping her distance. Not surprising. Little Ryan was, in a word, *adorable*. He clearly missed having a mother figure in his life. It was like he'd automatically imprinted on me and he'd taken to following me around the house when he wasn't in school. It was cute having him there chatting away as I sorted laundry or loaded the dishwasher.

I didn't mind at all. In fact it was kind of endearing, having him shadow me in his free time.

Right now, however, I was done with the Friday school drop off, the grocery run, and I had the whole house looking ship-shape. Top to bottom. Gray had given me free run of the place, including the master bedroom.

No way was I going up there, though. I even tried to stay away from the door to his private sanctuary.

Of course, a guy with this much money had a house-keeper who came in and did laundry and cleaning, so the job was pretty chilled out when I took all those things into account. I was responsible for the food for the kids, but that gave me control over the sugar intake, which was something I found out the hard way was better for me to oversee.

Children and sugar did not mix well, especially *these* children.

Gray ate with them whenever he was at home, but depending on his schedule, he sometimes ate special meals. And sometimes he ate my homemade macaroni and cheese because he couldn't resist it even though he was supposed to limit his carbohydrates that day.

With a free afternoon ahead of me and no one in the area I really wanted to see, I answered a text from Sophie, relieved when she wanted to meet for coffee.

It fit right into my perfectly empty schedule. I knew, though, there was a deeper meaning to the get-together. She wanted to see how I was doing, and I wanted some company over the age of eleven.

We picked a local place just down the street from the gated community and when I walked through the front door, I saw Sophie waiting for me, cradling the adorable Natalie on her lap.

I got in some quality snuggles with the baby girl as well, so I'd say my day was going pretty well indeed.

"Tell me, is my brother behaving himself?" Sophie asked as I sipped my caramel macchiato. I was a sucker for all things caramel, even if my hips wished that weren't the case.

"Yeah, he's been fine." I deliberately kept my answer as neutral as possible. She didn't need to know he was still Grumpy Gray on occasion. More often than not, I corrected.

Sophie smiled down at Natalie and continued to cradle

her close. "Did he tell you he'd expected a little old lady? The first day you got there?"

"What? No!" I replied loudly enough to earn a dirty look from the guy typing on his laptop at the next table.

"Yeah, I guess your old-fashioned name gave him the idea. So when *you*"—she waved her hand in my direction—"showed up, he nearly swallowed his tongue."

I chuckled at that. It certainly explained the weirdness of day one to me. And I found I kind of liked the idea. No way I'd tell Sophie, though. "Ah well, I hope he wasn't too disappointed," I said instead.

"I don't think *disappointed* was the word he'd have used." I wrinkled my brow in confusion and she continued with, "You're a gorgeous woman and even my monastic brother couldn't help but notice your assets. That's a good sign. He's been really shut off since Rachel died. I'm pleased to know he still has a pulse. Yes, he has a pulse! He does!" Sophie dropped into baby talk for the last bit, bending down to run her nose along Natalie's forehead. The baby laughed.

I shook my head. "Glad to be of service but I'm the nanny, Sophie. No good can come of fraternizing." *Or lusting.*

"Are you considering fraternizing?" she asked me.

From the innocent tone and rapid blinks I received, I knew that had been her whole idea in the first place. I *had* wondered why she'd hired me so quickly. Now I had my answer.

I wasn't usually one to lie, but sometimes, especially when I lied to myself as well, it was necessary. "He's not my type." At least I was being honest there. "I tend to go for nerdy, skinny guys, and I'm not long out of a pretty intense relationship. I'm not in the market to be fraternizing with anyone right now, especially not my brand-new boss."

She took a long, loud sip of her Frappuccino. "For the record, I find it admirable you want to wait. I've never exactly been great at turning off the physical desire tap. I mean, I wanted Lucky for *years*. Nonstop."

"This is not that. It's not what you and Lucky have," I clarified.

Sophie had told me a bit about her romance with the famous defenseman, enough to have the tiny remaining sliver of my hopeless romantic heart beating hard. Their story had seemed impossible and yet they were together today and happier than ever, no matter how many years passed or how much hope she'd lost.

"You don't think Gray's even a *bit* hot?" she pushed.

This girl was persistent. Her brother was tall, tanned, and muscular. He was all kinds of gruff and grumpy on the outside but sweet with his kids and clearly protective of those in his circle. And when he looked at me the way I sometimes caught him looking at me, my whole body heated up.

I wasn't going there.

"Objectively, sure. Still my boss, still not my type. Still not going there."

Sophie looked like she wanted to argue as I artfully changed the subject to something that felt a little less like having a magnifying glass held over my personal life.

I made it back to the house an hour later, just a *tiny* bit worked up thinking about Gray. Gray in his workout gear. Gray shoveling the breakfast I'd made into his mouth. Gray grumbling when the kids made a mess that he didn't want to clean up.

When I had pent-up energy like this, I preferred to

work it off through my music. It was a gorgeous October day. I swung open the doors to the pool house to let the fresh air in. Breathed deep.

Yes, there was no reason to keep this energy to myself. Not when my fingers twitched in anticipation.

I changed into a camisole and some casual shorts. I didn't want anything constraining me as I played. I wanted to feel alive and free and connected to the music. Hair loose, no constriction.

Opening the case was like reuniting with an old friend. The wood still shone from the last time I'd polished it. I drew out the bow and the rosin in preparation. I set the instrument against my left shoulder and adjusted my body into that old familiar position. It felt like coming home.

Then I set the strings on fire with the first draw of the bow.

I'd missed my violin, but stepping away from a life of music was easier than I'd thought. I had been hot-housed my whole life to be a violin virtuoso, and sure, I was good, I was *damn* good, some even said among the world's best. And I'd still lost the joy of playing in the end.

The need to be a certain person, seen in a certain way, had exhausted me. Playing music other people chose for me wore me down until I lost sight of *me*.

Who was Esther, really? What did *she* want?

When I was a kid, it hadn't occurred to me that I could have a say in what I played. It simply wasn't a part of my reality, and my parents certainly never encouraged me to use my talent to express myself. Violin was a discipline. I was to play well, sell tickets, and fill concert halls. I was one of those six-year-old child prodigies you'd see on stage, in a velvet dress and with a huge bow in my hair, playing at Carnegie Hall.

Yes, Carnegie Hall. That was my life from as early as I could remember.

Look the part, play to perfection, and sell out. Nothing more. As an adult I came to understand I was a product, a commodity people paid for. I'd never been allowed to simply be a child. I was too special. Too valuable.

In time, I'd tried to assert some control at least over the type of music I played, and still wherever I turned I was met with resistance. From my peers, from my handlers, from my parents. From my personal relationships. People wanted a certain version of me and nothing else.

In the end, I'd walked away rather than continue to have my life run by others.

In the open air of the pool house, I lost myself in the song and let myself go, my body moving sinuously and dancing with the music. It was a more modern piece, one I'd been toying with several times in the last few months to get right. My mother would hate it. But I really enjoyed it, a sexy song with an almost Latin cadence.

And living with Gray meant I had a whole lot of pent-up energy to throw into my interpretations. The next tune took on an almost erotic tone, and I continued to move with the violin. I closed my eyes and let the music guide me. I knew the piece by heart, so I didn't need to look at the music stand I'd set up. Even if a note or two was off, for once I didn't care. I played for myself, not for an audience. Not for a manager or conductor or my parents. I let myself play what I wanted to, the way I wanted to.

I shifted seamlessly to the next tune. Esther Richardson child prodigy was gone. This was Esther the soul musician. Esther the artist. Esther the woman who enjoyed her talent and her body because she didn't see the need to separate the two.

When I finished the last note, sweat dripped down my temples and between my ample breasts. My damp clothing clung to my body and I was spent, my breathing heavy. I lowered my instrument to its stand.

Then I heard the clapping.

Of course.

I knew who it had to be. I turned to see Gray standing in the open doorway. He wore a tight-fitting t-shirt with the Raiders logo and black shorts. He was barefoot.

I found the picture weirdly sexy. His hair was damp as if he'd just showered, pieces sticking up every which way. Adorably disheveled.

He looked at me with a kind of intensity I wasn't used to seeing on his face. Not when it came to me. I wasn't an unattractive woman but I'd spent my life in simple white shirts and black pencil skirts on stage, in demure dresses and pearls off. Much discussion took place around my weight and how I should try to shed it and keep it off. From my parents, my manager, *and* my ex. I'd always tried to hide my body or at least play it down. My outfits have never caused a man to look at me like he wanted to devour me.

Or maybe I'd been spending time with the wrong kind of men.

Gray's eyes raked over my body, taking in my legs and my waist and then the curve of my breasts beneath the cami. Which, much to my embarrassment, was wet with sweat and clinging to me. As his eyes trailed up and up, my traitorous nipples pebbled beneath the thin fabric.

I thought for the first time that maybe going braless under a white camisole was a bad choice.

"Wow, woman, you're so talented." He moved closer until he stood a few steps away from me. Not right in my space yet, but almost. Getting there.

Huh. He'd called me *woman* and suddenly that's how I felt. All woman. Strong and powerful and in control of myself for the first time. I stood up under his scrutiny with my hands on my hips. Waiting for...what?

"You may be one of the sexiest things I've ever seen," he continued. His tongue darted out to wet his lips and I followed the movement.

Oh.

Did he really just say that? I mean, I was pretty sure I heard him right but there's no way... Maybe I was imagining things. "Ah, thanks," I managed.

"I'm serious, Esther. You are amazing. Why aren't you a professional musician?" Gray took a step closer and the air seemed to be sucked out of the room. I couldn't breathe. "I bet I wouldn't be the only one who'd pay good money to listen to you play, and hell, I don't even understand music."

I laughed. Based on my conversation with Sophie that morning, it was pretty clear Gray hadn't even looked at my resume. He'd let Sophie do the hiring and had no idea about me or my background. It was kind of refreshing. Was this how he'd felt when I said I knew nothing about hockey? We were quite the ill-informed pair.

"I *was* a musician, actually, but I walked away from it. I was burnt out and I was never allowed to play the kind of music I wanted," I explained, tilting my head up to meet his eyes. "Thanks for the compliment, though."

Somehow, he'd moved forward without me realizing, taking up my space, close enough for me to reach up and touch. "Was it exactly like what you were doing here? The music you wanted to play, I mean."

He brushed a damp lock of hair off my forehead with his large hand and the touch sent a shiver of anticipation through my whole body. I had told Sophie I didn't want him in a sexual way. That was a lie. My body definitely did.

I don't really understand...

Gray wasn't my type. I'd almost exclusively dated only other musicians until now. My ex was the first chair viola. Before him, I was with a conductor. Men who wore tuxedos and had perfectly groomed hair and nails. They were thinkers, artists, not men whose job was physical in a way Gray's was.

They didn't work out for four and five hours a day. Instead, they used the time to practice and hone their craft, to perform impeccably.

Yet with Gray's eyes on me, the intensity in them and the way he clearly wanted me in this moment...well, I'd be a huge and terrible liar if I said it wasn't a mutual attraction.

"Yes. Exactly," I said. My voice didn't tremble. "I wanted to play modern music. I wanted to use my body, like a dance, as part of the performance. I'm a classical violinist and...as everyone says, that's not what they do. So when it became too much for me to handle anymore, all the rules, all the repression, I stepped away."

I'd also made a scene. I *couldn't* go back. But I kept that information to myself.

His eyes searched my face. He was looking for something, but I didn't know what. "And instead of playing, which is an absolute travesty, you're here being the world's sexiest nanny."

Wow. Heat curled low in my gut, and between my legs I could feel a different kind of wetness. This had definitely taken a different turn. Was it a turn for the worse?

Yes and no.

"I wouldn't say *world's* sexiest. Maybe top five," I

quipped, because we needed to defuse this bomb now before it went off.

Gray chuckled. It was a deep, rich, sexy rumble of a laugh that moved through his whole magnificent body. I'd heard him laugh a little with his kids and his buddies but nothing like this. The sound of Gray's genuine laughter was sexy and way too alluring for my good.

"Even though it's a very bad idea, I'm going to kiss you now, Esther."

The words were headier than I wanted to admit and more of a promise than a warning. I knew I should tell him no. I should in fact agree that this was a very bad idea and tell him to back away. Yet I did none of those things, no matter how my brain told me reality would be very different from what I had in mind.

I was curious to know what his lips would feel like on mine. What it would be like to have those huge arms corded around my body, and his firm chest pushed against mine. I wondered...would he bend down to grab me? Lift me up to him?

Would it be a languid, slow kiss or a fast and hungry one?

I wanted that kiss, so I held his gaze. My stomach flipped when he leaned down.

Gray's lips were an inch or two from mine.

We're doing this.

I craned in closer still, prepared to make what might be the worst decision yet—then his phone went off in his back pocket. We both pulled back as if we've been caught doing something naughty.

Which, in a way, we had been.

"School," he muttered before answering it. "Gray Wright."

I stepped away from him and moved to the small fridge in the room, grabbing myself a bottle of water. *Time to cool it down.* I took a sip and then held it to my chest as he finished the call. Gray didn't look happy.

"Ryan is sick. Vomiting. I have to go get him." His eyes shifted toward me again from across the room. They were on my breasts specifically and I realized I was almost naked in front of him.

Weirdly, I made no move to cover myself. I liked the way he looked at me. My already pebbled nipples hardened further under his gaze.

God, there must be something wrong with my head.

"Do you want me to get him?" I offered.

He shook his head. As if trying to shake clear the image of me. I couldn't help the cutting slice of anxiety at the thought. "You can...get dressed. I have a feeling things won't be too pretty when I get home."

"I'll do that. See you when you get back."

Neither of us mentioned the almost-kiss and he moved to go. I headed for the shower. I'd be doing everything I could to cool off before he and his sick son came home. That's why I was here, I reminded myself, to look after the kids.

Yes, Gray was hot. And sure, there was an attraction between us. I'd be lying if I didn't admit to finding it flattering, but we were going to have to ignore it.

Whether we liked it or not.

7

GRAY

Damn me. It'd been ten hours since I nearly kissed Esther. Ten hours since I almost gave in to those urges I'd, until now, been able to master. To shove down deep and ignore on my good days and fight against on the bad ones.

I wasn't sure what had changed inside of me or where my famous resolve disappeared to, but I needed it back ASAP. Luckily, the choice had been taken out of my hands.

First it was Ryan. He was green when I picked him up from school, and instead of heading home right away, I'd gotten another call and had to make a brief detour. Make that calls, plural. Georgie was puking. Violently. Oh, and Candace too. Both of them were in the nurse's office waiting for me.

Time to go and get them as well.

It must have been something they'd eaten, the doctor told me when I made an emergency appointment for the three; they needed rest and fluids and then they'd be fine.

If three kids vomiting their guts up wasn't a sign from the universe to try and stop me from making a bad move, then I had no idea what was. It seemed pretty clear-cut to me.

Esther was a big no-no.

No matter how parts of me felt when I looked at her. Physical chemistry was not a good enough reason for me to slip up and make a mistake right now, or so I tried to convince myself.

Tonight, I found myself on my hands and knees with a bucket of diluted bleach at my side and a toothbrush. Yes, toothbrush. I scrubbed the tiles around the toilet until they gleamed because when you have kids, you step up. Every part of me wanted to give in to the exhaustion riding me, but—

You do the dirty stuff yourself and you take care of business.

Business often included cleaning up puke from the worst places imaginable. And my kids? They weren't content to keep to one space alone. They managed to not only trash their bathroom but my own as well.

Thanks, guys.

I couldn't blame them. It wasn't their fault they were sick and throwing up everywhere. Including my shoes. Still, it sucked.

Speaking of sucking...

My mind took another dive into the gutter where it so often wanted to go these days.

So far, there had been *nothing* sexy about what Esther and I went through together in the last ten hours. Stress and bodily fluids and screaming kids didn't exactly spell romance. And yet every time I thought about her, thought about watching her work the violin with such passion and the way her lithe body moved—

Yup, there I went again. Hard even while cleaning the toilet. I glared down at my traitorous erection.

I needed to get a grip on myself. I closed my eyes and took a moment to breathe, picturing the ice. My routine before I went out there to lead my team. Did I let the guys get away with this kind of nonsense? I'd had my fair share of rounding up heartsick rookies and slapping sense into them when they got in their own heads. It affected their game.

Why did I have such a difficult time doing the same thing for myself?

"Get a grip," I muttered. Staring at the porcelain. "Get your head in the right space and stop being stupid."

The right space being...what? Working out, killing it on the ice when the season started in two days, and being the best dad I could be. None of those things included fantasizing about my nanny.

It was time to stop acting like a lovesick fool and start acting like the man in charge.

I finally finished up the cleaning and chucked the toothbrush right in the garbage. My knees ached when I rose and, glancing out toward the master bedroom, I saw the bed. Rising further I made out the three shapes snuggled beneath the blankets, their limbs tangled. My heart melted staring at them.

Candace was in the middle, sprawled on her back, with Ryan to her left curled in a fetal position. Georgia took up more than her fair share of space even on her side. Her legs were spread like she was prepared to jump over a track hurdle.

Even with a king-size bed there would be little room available for me.

Part and parcel with the job description, although I did wonder how much it would cost for a custom bed larger than a king. Did they make those? I might do an internet search tomorrow. Tonight, I was way too tired.

I dumped the bucket of bleach down the shower drain and washed my hands.

Legs shaking, I sat in one of the chairs Rachel had picked out, the gas-burning fireplace sleeping like the children.

Life was strange, I thought. You start out thinking your life is going in one direction and then you meet a woman, you sign a contract, and things change. Boom. You're on the ice with cameras in your face and adrenaline pumping. Your wife announces her pregnancy and boom, things change again. Suddenly there is a little tiny human who needs things. Needs *you*. Candace was so small and help-less, red and wriggling. Crying constantly.

Then suddenly there was Georgia. And Ryan.

And cancer.

Cancer had by far been the biggest game changer because I'd finally settled into the picture of my life when it showed up. I knew who I was and what I wanted. I knew how to provide for my family and actually had fun doing it.

Then everything was different. Everything changed and I found myself living in the hospital with Rachel. Sophie took time out of her young budding life to care for the kids for me while I sat with my wife.

For what? To lose her in the end anyway. To have the game changed again because boom, I was a widower now.

I stared at nothing as Esther snuck into the room on quiet feet. She didn't spare me a glance before moving to the bed and dabbing the wet washcloth she carried over the kids' foreheads. Loose slacks hid most of her assets from view, thankfully. I didn't need to get worked up this late.

Soothing hands pushed Candace's hair away from her

face before moving on to the other children.

"This was quite a day, Puck Daddy," Esther whispered loud enough for me to hear her.

Puck Daddy? It sounded strange coming from her and I chuckled. "I guess you heard the nickname somewhere, huh?"

Esther nodded but her face was a mask. I couldn't tell if she was amused or not, and I didn't want to ask her opinion.

"Yes, it was definitely quite the shit show," I agreed.

Her lips pursed. "I think you mean puke show. Nothing we can't handle. At least they're getting some rest now."

"Thank you for today," I continued. My fingers knotted on my lap. "I couldn't have done this alone. You were so strong." She'd stood by them through every episode, holding their hair, getting them water and crackers and soothing them when they started to cry. She'd rubbed Ryan's stomach until he stopped complaining about how much it hurt.

"You have to be."

"My first time changing a diaper? I almost emptied my guts. I didn't seem to get over my reaction until Ryan was born and I didn't have a choice anymore. It wasn't fair to push everything on my wife. How did *you* know what to do?"

Esther let out a sigh. "My last family? Food poisoning. I'm no stranger to messy situations and there is nothing messier than stomach issues. You can't get upset or sick over these things because the kids need you."

Hadn't I said almost the same thing?

Without Esther, I would have been frantic, calling in whatever favor I could with my sister to get her to unwrap herself from Lucky's arms and come over. To give myself someone to lean on when I wanted to fall apart, too.

That's what they don't tell you when you lose a spouse. It's like having a limb cut off unexpectedly. If you can't afford a new one, if you're plain unlucky, if you don't have support from friends and family, things are off balance. You fall.

I'd tried so damn hard not to fall because my kids needed me. How do you balance a high-profile career and a daily routine when you're missing a limb?

"Well...thank you."

"You don't need to thank me," she said.

"You have no idea how much it means to me, having you here." *With me.*

Esther shot me a small smile and sat carefully on the edge of the bed so she wouldn't disturb the children. "That's why I'm here. I'm here to help you."

"That's why I pay you."

Her smile remained in place as she faced me and I thought I saw a small crack in her armor. Had my words struck a chord?

I clicked a button on a remote. The gas fireplace lit with a crack and a spark. I didn't know why I needed the comfort of the flames between us, the light and heat and sound, but I did.

"What made you get into nannying in the first place?"

The look on her face at the question told me to be careful how deep I probed tonight.

"It's a long and boring story. I'm not sure you actually want to hear it right now," she answered slowly.

"Maybe some other time?"

"Let's say there were things about my childhood I wished I could change. Things I wanted for myself that circumstances didn't permit. I won't get into the circumstances except to say it wasn't ideal and I missed out on a few things." Esther paused, twisting her hands on her lap. She glanced over at the kids.

My attention immediately went to the elegant curve of her neck, the delicate profile and flawless jaw. Even this early in the morning, the pitch-black outside making me feel like we were the only two people in the world, she looked pretty. Exhausted, but beautiful.

"I think everyone has pieces of their past they wish they could change," I said. I thought about Rachel and the cancer, how I would take away her pain and the kids' pain if I had the chance. "The only thing we can do is focus on the moment and make the best of our time."

Esther's smile was bright enough to light the darkness. "Yes, true."

I didn't want to talk about the elephant in the room. It would be there whether I ignored it or not. That almost kiss. The way her breath caught in her throat just a little when I had leaned in to claim her lips.

The sign from the universe keeping us apart before we even started. I really believed it.

"About before..." I trailed off. Dared to glance up at her and wondered what she saw when she looked at me. Esther's gaze didn't falter. I didn't want to say it.

She said it for me. "About before.... I think we should keep things as they are, Gray."

"Huh?" My brows drew together.

"There's no reason for us to complicate things by moving in a direction where we aren't sure how it will go." She paused again and kept her gaze focused solely on the children. Her lips drew apart in a small sigh and my mind instantly shot back to the almost kiss. "It's better for me if things remain as they are...with us."

Better for her? Wow. That hurt more than I expected. It

took work to keep my face neutral. "I feel the same way," I repeated dully.

"Exactly. I'm glad to hear it. As you said, you pay me to be here. The balance has already been set between us and nothing but trouble comes from upsetting the balance. You're a good-looking man." The chuckle was back and I wondered at the ease in which she made the statement. "I'll get it out there before we go further. I find you very handsome. It doesn't change the job I'm here to do for you or the reality of our current situation. Things have to stay the same."

"Agreed," I barked out.

Then quickly caught myself when Ryan stirred, groaning in his sleep.

Esther rose from the bed and went into the bathroom to wet the washcloth again. She returned a few seconds later, bending over Georgie to wipe her forehead.

"I'm going downstairs to get them something to drink." Esther straightened and shook out her shoulders. "Once they wake up, make them take a sip, even if their stomachs aren't in good shape. It will help replenish what they lost."

"I know."

It came out as pissed as I felt. I didn't rise from the chair when Esther walked out of the room.

This was what I'd wanted. Right? I'd said pretty much the same thing in my mind on repeat. Why did it sting so much coming out of her mouth? She agreed. We were on the same page.

She didn't want to push and move things forward, which was great.

So I did what any man in my situation would do. I spent the next week avoiding her.

8

ESTHER

The start of hockey season began the following week and I took the kids to the first game, as Gray had warned me I'd be expected to do. It was a home game against some East Coast team whose name I could not for the life of me remember.

They were up and out of bed with the first light of dawn, and though I went through the motions of coffee and breakfast, I felt myself keeping on the lookout for Gray. When I didn't hear a peep out of him, Candace assured me he'd left at four in the morning to get to the rink with the others. It was their ritual.

I couldn't say I was excited for my first NHL romp; rather I was more eager to see what all the fuss was about, more interested to see how Gray and his friends were on the ice together. I guess I was more interested in a glimpse into their world than the game itself.

Ice, definitely not *grass* or *turf*. I'd learned my lesson after much merciless teasing.

Since their sickness, the kids had been...better with me. The girls especially were better and kinder and a little less aloof than when we first met. It was the most amazing feeling to watch them slowly come out of their shells.

Candace had such a capacity for giving, even if she didn't want anyone to know it. I'd seen her step in multiple times with her younger siblings and steer them away from a potential mishap, only to see me watching and write it off like nothing happened.

Georgia was quite the artist. She had a way with paints that certainly seemed a step beyond most others in her age group. She wasn't shy about using any medium or surface at her disposal, either. Including the walls. I didn't think Aunty Sophie had been what anyone would call strict. When Georgia wasn't painting, her sweet little nose was buried in a book.

And Ryan...well, he had taken to me easily. I'd never seen a sweeter little boy.

Their daddy, on the other hand?

Their daddy had been avoiding me and we both knew it.

He liked to play it off as being *busy* whenever I made a tiny comment about his absence. Once he even reminded me that this was what happened when the season started and I shouldn't expect to see him around much. There was no doubt he was busy.

I knew the truth. I knew what avoidance looked like. At least, I thought I knew the truth. Which didn't make any sense, because we'd talked about keeping the status quo and seemed to both be on the same page. He was worried he might have fucked things up between us. Ha! If only he knew.

Do I wish we'd at least gotten the chance to kiss? To feel his lips on mine, caressing and nibbling? To see how he tasted? Yes. Of course!

I hadn't been lying when I told him I found him attractive. Only a blind woman wouldn't want Gray Wright.

However, we both seemed to understand we were playing with fire if we went down that road. I was the nanny. He was my boss. End of story, close the book and burn it. I had no intention of stepping over a line that was there for a reason.

It was a line I wouldn't cross no matter how handsome, how desirable he was.

And anyway, he wasn't my type, I reminded myself for the thousandth time. Gorgeous and muscled and sexually attractive were some big red flags in my book. They had been ever since—

Well. That was then. This was now.

"Come on, guys, we're going to be late," I said as I hustled the kids toward Gray's SUV which he'd told me to drive whenever I had the kids. When alone I still preferred my pink Mini. They were bundled up like we were facing the dead of winter rather than a mildly pleasant October day. "We won't be able to find a good parking spot if we dawdle."

Candace rolled her eyes at me before claiming the front seat. "We're the captain's kids. We'll always have a parking spot. *Duh.*"

Her tone definitely let me know that I should have considered this before speaking. Maybe I should have, but my nerves were wreaking havoc and made it kind of hard for me to focus on logic. Nerves about seeing Gray in action.

"Okay, fine." I blew out a breath. "Good to know. Still, there is sure to be traffic and we don't want to be late."

There were going to be some serious things to relearn on this journey, I thought as I pulled down the driveway and took the winding streets out of the gated community. Some serious things. Keeping an open mind would help.

I took the roads at the speed limit, relying on the kids to guide me in the right direction. I didn't know where the rink was or how to get there, having been completely in the dark in terms of anything to do with the NHL.

Luckily, Candace was right about the parking spot and despite the awful crowd of vehicles packed around the arena, she pointed me toward a space reserved for the Wrights. The passes we flashed at the gatehouse helped as well.

I should have known. Privilege came with position. It wasn't a lesson I thought I'd easily forget and yet here we were. I guess I needed the reminder.

Get yourself together, girl, I said to my reflection in the mirror.

She said nothing back. Typical. She was always silent when I needed advice.

"Come on, this way."

Ryan grabbed my hand on the way inside and tugged me toward the box where the players' friends and families sat. The temperature dropped a good ten degrees once the doors closed.

The interior of the arena reminded me so much of when I used to travel with the Symphony, except rougher. Until we moved past the concession stands into general admission. Ahead, the ice gleamed, a pristine surface of white recently polished and ready for the players.

No wonder some people compared it to a barn.

"I'm going to go ahead and assume we don't have to worry about finding a seat, either," I said to the kids.

Candace rolled her eyes again—a move she'd certainly

inherited from her father—and Georgia rushed ahead to show me exactly where we'd be sitting.

"It's this way, Esther," she said. "Watch your step. Okay? You don't want to fall."

Wow, there were a lot of people here for the game. Way more than I would have expected, but then again, people love sports. Hockey must be a pretty big deal around here. I'd forgotten how it felt to be surrounded by such life. Such energy. It was a force unto itself.

The moment we arrived at the private box, all eyes were on us. On *me*. I squirmed for a good minute before straightening my shoulders. Oh, boy. I was used to the stares from being onstage all those years. I was used to the nasty glances because of my ex and his groupies. Since hockey had puck bunnies, would cellists have string foxes? I was still working on a name.

This was a completely new level for me. Some of the women in these seats were giving off seriously hostile vibes. And for what? They didn't know me from Eve and yet somehow I seemed to have a bright red target painted right between my eyes.

My grip on Ryan's hand tightened imperceptibly.

"My, my," one of them said with a sneer. "Looks like we've got some fresh meat over here, girls."

I ignored the strange woman.

"Esther! Over here. Hi guys, how are ya?"

Sophie's sweet voice filtered through the echoing noise of the arena and I hurried toward her, trying not to look and feel like she was my lifeline. My boots skidded a little on the cement risers.

"Go on, kids, find your seats. The game is about to start. Hi, sweetheart!" Sophie rose to give Georgia a hug before shooing them into whatever chairs she'd marked as theirs.

They didn't seem particularly upset about the seating order so I'd go ahead and assume, again, they knew exactly where to go. This was old hat to them.

And wow, I was glad they'd warned me to dress accordingly. It was cold this close to the ice and already I saw my breath gusting in a white cloud in front of my face.

How long did these games last and how long would I be expected to sit? Sports had never appealed to me. Beyond the genuine curiosity to see what my new boss did for a living, I didn't much care for the rest of the festivities.

"Well, hey." Sophie drew out the word. She patted the seat next to her and stared expectantly at me. Her long hair was pulled up behind her in a twisted bun and I noticed then how her scarf matched her gloves in a merry shade of maroon. "How is it going?"

I told her, "Fine. It's fine."

She swallowed a laugh, her attention on the players' box. "Fine," she repeated with only a hint of mockery. "Sounds like there's a lot you want to say and too many prying ears around to tell me the truth. Also, ignore those women. Especially Brittney. She's kind of known as the resident crazy bitch around here."

I suspected Sophie pretty much hit the nail on the head there. "It's fine!" I insisted, smiling. Tugging on the end of my own ponytail. "I know we're all excited to watch the game today."

The arena seats were crowded with fans wearing the team's signature colors. There were jerseys and flags and vendors walking in between the rows hawking food and drinks.

So very different from the crowds I knew. I remembered looking out at the arenas before the symphony played, at the hidden enthusiasm and the well-dressed men and women seated there with nothing but decorum to keep them warm.

Here, the fans wore their enthusiasm on display. There were even a few rowdy guys who'd ripped off their shirts to reveal their painted bodies with the team's colors of black, purple, and green. They howled the loudest.

The team mascot skated out onto the ice with his furry fox arms raised to drum up enthusiasm. From this vantage point I could see the players in their own box, with Gray standing near the door to the ice giving what I assumed was a pep talk.

"There is going to be a lot of yelling and a lot of name-calling," Sophie warned me. "Definitely a lot of cursing because once the guys get out there, I don't know, they turn into some kind of weird primal cavemen and all they can do to express themselves is to shout obscenities. Or grunt. I have an extra pair of ear buds if you want them. I know it can be a little loud when you aren't used to the din."

"Sort of like it was for the cookout?" I asked as a joke.

"Imagine the cookout amplified by a thousand. Except these are grown-ass adults. So, yeah. Much worse. Also, there are often fights but Gray is unlikely to be involved."

At least the kids looked settled. They were used to this kind of action. I was the newbie here. I tugged at the jersey I'd gotten out of the laundry, a way for me to show my support. It must be one of Gray's because it was way too big for any of the kids. Hopefully he didn't mind me borrowing it for the first game.

"I might take you up on the ear buds," I told Sophie.

My sentence was lost in the sound of the buzzer over-head to signal the start of the game. In some distant part of my head, I knew the announcers were speaking, cataloguing the players' stats and signature moves while both teams moved out onto the ice.

Okay, apparently it was time for this circus to start. I rubbed my hands together when the tips of my fingers felt a little chilled.

I'd wanted to ask Sophie more about the other players' wives and girlfriends, the ones currently boring holes in the back of my head because I sat in the first row, so I could at least get a better handle on the women glaring at me and why. I wanted to know why that woman, Brittney, was considered the resident crazy bitch. There had to be a good backstory to go along with her title.

The moment the game took off, my attention splintered.

Fast. Loud. Violent. It was hard to keep track of who was who beneath the masks. I took to trying to follow the numbers on the jerseys.

Number 11. Lucky Price. Sophie's man, the Raiders' defender.

Number 26. Dominik. He was easy to spot as the goalie. He didn't leave his post.

Number 3. Gray Wright, the team captain. "Puck Daddy" leading the play and his people in a well-organized unit against the opposition. Once I found Gray on the ice, I had to admit...it was sexy.

Very *weirdly* sexy because I never would have imagined razor-sharp skates and huge padding a turn-on. He stopped on a dime with ice scattering behind him, his large hands hidden in mitts, gripping the stick tightly.

How could I get so hot by simply watching him?

He glided like it took no effort at all to move his body. His gear hid most of his body from view but still he was attractive as hell.

Red flag, red flag!

I needed to remember our almost-kiss and why it was still a terrible idea to get involved with him. The whys of it hadn't changed, no matter how good he looked when he skated.

There was a tug at my elbow and when I looked over, Ryan had switched seats with Sophie.

"What's the matter?" I asked him. Loudly, to be heard above the din. "Are you all right?"

"My dad is the team leader. There are six players on the ice at all times, including him. You see those guys in front of the nets? Those are the goalies. Their job is to make sure the puck doesn't get past them," he explained in a high, sweet voice.

"Ah. I think I understand."

Ryan went on to explain the rules of hockey to me with as much detail as his five-year-old brain understood about the game.

My heart melted even further. He leaned close, speaking directly next to my ear and taking me through the moves, positions, and the responsibilities of each player. His father had said Candace was the hockey fan but I had to wonder if he wasn't wrong about that.

I was so caught up in what Ryan was saying that I didn't notice Gray go down. I didn't notice it when the center for the opposite team rammed a shoulder into him and sent him flying across the ice. I did notice when his helmet slammed into the side of the rink with a resounding clunk, his head snapping into the ice.

The arena erupted in a chorus of boos. I found myself on my feet, hands tense, knees locked.

"Gray!"

Sophie's cry cut through my own panic at seeing him lying there. Glancing over, I tugged a white-faced Ryan to my side and gestured to Georgia and Candace that it was okay.

It was okay.

Right?

The referee called for a pause and several attendants and bench players came to take Gray off the ice. He didn't move as they dragged him away from the rink.

"Oh my God. What happened?"

Had I actually said that out loud?

I must have looked pretty shaky. I felt shaky. Was he going to be okay? My chest dissolved into a mass of knots.

The next thing I knew, Sophie had ahold of my shoulder. "Go on back and see him for yourself. This kind of thing happens all the time but it can be a little jarring when you aren't used to it."

So why did her face look pale, too?

"I'm not sure what I would do back there," I said with a shake of my head.

"Doesn't matter. Sometimes the best thing to do is to see with your own eyes that he's fine. I'll take care of the kids. Go on."

I wasn't going to argue with her. I knew from the look on her face she was dead set on sending me back, and I left the box with one hand over my stomach.

This is all part of the game, I tried to tell myself. My mind recalled the moment Gray's head cracked against the side of the rink, replaying in a loop in my brain.

Fumbling in my pocket, I grabbed the all-access pass Gray had given me before he left for the game. The plastic felt strange and cold in my hand as I hurried...where? Where did I even go? I found one of the arena stewards—what were they called?—waiting by the exit and flashed my pass at him.

"I need to see Gray Wright. Here. I've got...I've got a pass."

He didn't ask questions and he didn't think twice before gesturing for me to follow him. My footsteps sounded rushed even to my ears but soon we were standing in front of a bright red door marked PRIVATE.

The locker room?

I had no clue but pushed ahead anyway. I still had a lot to learn, obviously.

The knot in my chest grew larger until I found it difficult to breathe.

"Gray?" I called out.

The room was empty but a low murmur of voices came from further back. I ignored the equipment scattered across the floor and picked my way toward the sound.

"I'm sorry, miss, you can't be back here."

A hand fell on my shoulder and only the squeeze of fingers could have kept me from pushing ahead.

Turning around, I saw a woman in a white coat staring me down, territorial.

"I'm here to see Gray Wright," I said weakly.

"I'm sorry, you aren't allowed back here even with your pass, Miss."

"I'm his live-in girlfriend."

The lie left my lips smoothly and later, much later, I'd wonder why it didn't bother me at all.

The doctor, or whatever she was, stared at me for a moment longer with her lips pursed before nodding. "All right, then. Follow me."

My head hurt like a mother.

I hated that I was lying on a table while my team was on the ice without me.

I'm the captain. I'm supposed to be out there.

Even if I was only on the sidelines, where I also hated hanging out, it was better than feeling useless. The hit came out of nowhere and before I knew it, stars. Stars dancing behind my closed lids when my head collided with the side of the rink. Even now my eyes were crossed, struggling to focus.

One of my hardest hits, I thought. Maybe ever. Things were blurry and didn't seem to be clearing up quickly enough. Damn the other defender for his full-body slam. He'd known what he was doing with the hit.

"I said to keep still!" The doctor—better known as Nicole Stewart, or Doc Nicole—put a hand on my chest to keep me from squirming. The woman had one hell of a grip and I eventually stopped fighting her. "You're so stubborn. You don't listen."

Doc Nicole wouldn't even let me have the TV on

because she wanted me to rest my eyes. I'd rest later: the game was on *now*. I knew she was just doing her job, but it still stung, maybe more than my head. Which, as I said, really *did* hurt.

"Are you going to behave?" Nicole questioned.

I groaned. "Why are you talking to me like I'm a child?"

"Because you're acting like one. Now, *are you going to behave*? I shouldn't have to ask you again."

I tried to nod and immediately regretted the movement when pain pinged from my head down my spine. "Yes, doc. I'll stay still."

"Good. I'll be right back."

She stepped out of the room, no doubt because she was sick of talking to my grumpy ass and needed a break. I couldn't blame her for wanting one. I'd try to be less of a tool when she returned.

I slowly raised my hands to my head, rubbing until the ache was too much and I had to relax again. I always insisted that all our team players maintained focus during a game. Myself included. This game was no exception. Then again, I knew *she* was watching.

Esther.

And while I'd tried my hardest not to think about Esther in the stands or what she was wearing or what she thought of the game, I did. A lot. I had spotted her in a Raiders jersey and I was pretty sure it was mine. I loved how she'd done that.

She knew nothing about hockey, and I wanted her if not to like it then to at least respect what I did, so to see her in my jersey...it meant a lot.

It was a weird thing to want to earn someone's respect. I hadn't wanted to or needed to for a long time.

As an NHL star, people tended to treat me like I was

special, if only because I'd gotten lucky enough to sign with and lead a great team of people. I got the best seats in restaurants when I went out to eat, better service than the tables around me, fair or not. And women, well, they were more than available to me.

Not that I wanted them.

Of course, I'd earned some of those perks due to how well I played, but sometimes I was treated to a different standard simply because I was famous.

Esther didn't see me the same way. I was just her boss. Or the guy who flirted with her, depending on the situation. It mattered to me how she saw what I did and how hard I worked. The real me instead of the public persona.

I closed my eyes for a minute and the doctor's voice sounded from beside me.

"Hey, Gray. I've got your *live-in girlfriend* here to see you. Are you cool with a visitor?"

Oh, the smugness in Doc Nicole's voice. It was unmistakable.

I popped one eye open and then the other, instantly regretting it when my pain tripled. What was that about a live-in girlfriend? I knew I had a bad bump to the head but I was pretty sure I didn't have a special woman when I went out on the ice.

This intriguing turn of events brought a small smile to my face and I immediately agreed. "Absolutely."

Esther walked into the room and approached the exam table with a very worried expression on her pretty face. "Gray? Are you okay?"

At once I felt bad now that I'd spent *days* avoiding her. Given how anxious she looked, I knew the feeling would soon shift into guilt, embarrassment. An apology. "Worried about me?"

Her lower lip began to wobble.

It'd been a long time since I'd had anyone worry about me. Rachel had been gone three years and we found out she was sick when she was pregnant with our son. There were too many other things to consider besides myself, and I'd felt selfish speaking up. So, more than five years had passed since I was the actual recipient of someone's worry and not the one doing the worrying.

It felt...nice, to say the least. Better than nice. It felt kind of awesome to have someone care about me. I mean, the kids cared, of course, but I tended to play this kind of stuff down for them because they'd dealt with enough.

"I'm fine, Esther," I said finally, taking in those curves in her tight-fitting jeans and ankle boots. Her dark hair was pulled up in a ponytail, making her look young and sexy.

The jersey revealed more of her long neck and I wanted to kiss my way down it towards— *Not now,* I reminded myself. *Bad timing, Gray.*

Then, remembering how we had company and hamming it up for the doc's benefit, I reached out a hand for Esther. "I've got a bump on the head. Come here and kiss it better, baby. Please."

She gave a small eye roll at my performance but she took my hand regardless, and hers was icy-cold from sitting by the rink. To my surprise she did come closer, closer yet, and I took advantage by bringing her down for a kiss that escalated fast.

Talk about seizing the opportunity. I hadn't been planning on it until she'd touched me.

But I was injured, not dead. And for the last few days, this was all I'd wanted to do but I couldn't, so I seized the opportunity to sweep my tongue against hers. Much to my surprise, she didn't put up a fight.

My first taste of her.

I tasted soda and popcorn and Esther. Her chest pressed into my side and I felt her soft curves. I slid one hand into her hair and placed the other on the small of her back, drawing her ever closer. It was a slow, deep kiss that had me hard beneath the flimsy medical blanket.

This was what I'd wanted the other day after watching her play her violin. *This* was the kiss we'd put off pretty much since our first meeting.

I wanted it to last forever. She was sweet, so much sweeter than I'd bargained for, her lips plump and soft.

I wouldn't have minded stripping Esther naked and taking her there in the doc's small office beneath the arena. In fact, *that* fantasy would now join the very long list of fantasies I'd gathered in my head, all involving the woman whose lips were pushed against mine right now.

Such as...

Esther in my bed begging me to make her come. Esther naked in the pool. Taking Esther from behind in the kitchen. Esther and I together in the outdoor shower... Those were a few of my favorites.

"You scared me," she whispered against my lips before pulling back. "I didn't know what to think." Her fingers trailed along my jaw. "You went down on the ice so hard and I panicked. You hurt yourself."

The doctor cleared her throat. Apparently, the show was over before it really began.

What a damn shame.

"You'll be fine, Mr. Wright. Too bad it's game over for you today," Nicole told me.

Hell, I'd known that since the moment I hit the side of the rink; this wasn't my first rodeo. Or professional hockey game.

I groaned at the news before the doc turned her focus on Esther. "Since you're the girlfriend I've never heard about, I'm going to relay this to you since he's too stuff-eared to pay attention to me. He needs to be watched all night. Head injuries are serious, I can't stress that enough. Ignore anything he tells you to the contrary. Keep a close watch on him," Nicole instructed Esther. "These guys are all terrible patients. The worst I've had to deal with in my entire career!"

"Hey now!" I protested to Nicole, but honestly, she was not wrong.

None of us liked being injured and none of us ever really wanted to take the time to heal. The ice was our life, and we wanted to be on it, always. This head injury was going to take me out of commission for longer than I was willing to give. But I knew better than to push myself. Not with three kids to take care of.

Esther had her back to me as she listened to Doc Nicole, so I rested my hand on her hip. I *finally* had my hands on that lush body and there was no way I'd let go until I absolutely had to. My eyes drifted up and I smiled at the name on the jersey she wore. #3 Wright.

Yup, it was one of mine. I'd known it.

Seeing it in front of me, however, did things to me it shouldn't. I added seeing Esther in nothing but my jersey to the fantasy list. Lusting after the nanny, maybe even detailed thoughts of sex with the nanny was fine, I tried to console myself. Anything more was not in the cards for us...

"Don't worry, I'll keep him in line," Esther was saying in her firm, no-nonsense nanny voice. It was the one she used on the girls when they pushed her too far.

It was sexy as fuck. Yeah, I had it bad for my employee, I thought as I tightened my grip on her. Maybe she didn't feel quite the same way. Still, she *had* kissed me like she did. I would take that as a very positive sign.

Sophie and the kids burst into the room before I could say or do anything else. I let my hand drop away from Esther and instantly regretted it. *She* immediately stepped aside to allow the kids access, while reminding them to be gentle.

"Daddy's going to be all right, guys. Don't worry," she finished.

Sophie whispered something to her. Something I probably did not want to know, and Esther nodded before saying, "I promise."

"You good, bro?" Sophie asked over my kids' heads. Although the three of them stormed me, all talking above the others, I gave her a thumbs-up because nodding my head still hurt.

"I'm fine," I told them all firmly.

"Listen to Esther. Whatever she says goes. Don't make me come over and kick your ass." Sophie mimed making a fist and using it on me. "You know I will."

"Language around the kids," Esther reminded her gently.

Which almost made me want to laugh because I knew for certain my kids heard way worse than that in the stands, but she was right.

I smiled. One minute she was so prim and proper and the next she was hot and sexy. All part of what drew me to her. She was not one thing or one dimension. She was a whole lot of uniqueness in a gorgeous package.

And she tasted *so sweet*.

Sophie waved her off, and after asking the children if they were okay now that they'd seen me, she made her way toward the door. She probably wanted to get back out there and watch Lucky on the ice for the rest of the game.

"Let's wait outside while your father gets dressed," Esther said, ushering the kids after their aunt. "He's going to be all right. I promise."

Worry still colored her voice, however.

"Don't forget, eyes on this one all night," Doc Nicole reminded her.

Esther bit her lip and my stomach flipped. Was she actually nervous about staying up with me all night? Hmm. Smart girl. Biting her lip in that sexy way? Not so smart if she wanted to deter me.

"No problem, doc," Esther answered with a confidence she didn't feel. I could tell.

Nicole was the last person to leave the room, turning around to look at me with an I-mean-business glare.

As I got dressed, I thought about the kiss. It was amazing. Delicious. And I wanted to do it again. Everyone had already warned me about how stupid it was to pursue anything with Esther, and they were right. It was foolish and reckless and a whole lot of other things I couldn't think about.

I paused for a moment, wincing at the flash of pain in my head. When was the last time I'd done anything *truly* reckless?

It had to be years ago, before Rachel got sick. That was a long time for anyone to play by the rules, to take no chances, but especially for a guy like me.

I was not *this guy* by nature. Sure, I was wild when I was young. I took risks. As long as I could get back up and on the ice, the next day it didn't matter. That was my rule for myself. I played as hard as I worked, as long as I actually *got up* the next day and did what I needed to do.

I didn't become Puck Daddy at age twenty-two because I was cautious, I thought with a laugh, pulling the rest of my hoodie down to cover my torso.

My wife and I had both liked to party back then. Heck, we were just kids. I'd slept with Rachel without protection more than once and we made Candace, but neither of us shied away from the responsibility. Work hard, play hard, and Rachel had agreed. We were a team. We had each other's back. Even after we married and our baby was born, I still did crazy things. Diving with sharks, hang gliding, riding the mechanical bull...I did it all. That's who I was.

Until my wife died and left me to raise our three kids on my own.

Then I became the guy who cut the crusts off of sandwiches and sang lullabies and resisted all temptation. Who took no unnecessary risks if they involved potential threat or harm to my family. I was a responsible father and I worked really hard to be him.

Yet I was alone. Not lonely, exactly, but alone nonetheless.

After years of being sensible, did I want to be a little reckless and go after Esther? I absolutely did.

Was it selfish of me? I wondered as I pulled on my boots, stars dancing behind my eyes again. Probably, but just this once, Puck Daddy was going to get a little of what *he* wanted, and the consequences be damned.

10

ESTHER

It felt like hours since I'd seen Gray lying there on that examination table, looking half dead after his ordeal on the ice. Gosh, what a scary experience. One I never wanted to repeat for the rest of my days.

Even now, my hands shook and the moment replayed over and over again in my head. I was terrified something had happened to him, and as much as I didn't want to admit it, it was in more than an employee–employer capacity. Still, I wondered if I could keep this job and avoid hockey altogether. Probably not.

And the kiss—

He'd taken advantage of the moment. Clearly. Yet I hadn't said *no* or pulled away. I'd wanted the kiss for days, maybe not under those circumstances but I had wanted to be kissed by Gray.

Several times that night, as I was getting the kids in and out of the car, their pajamas on, their teeth cleaned, I'd caught myself with my fingers to my lips. Remembering what it felt like to be kissed. I'd told him *no* the first time he attempted the kiss, even as my body demanded we find out what he would feel like, how he would taste.

Now I knew. I suppressed a giggle.

For the record, it had felt good. So damn good. I wondered what would have happened if the doctor hadn't been there to stop us from going further. I should probably be down on my knees thanking Nicole for her mere presence.

I sighed, feeling like a kid again. When was the last time a kiss had gotten me so excited? Um, probably never. At least, no one time I could remember.

And there was no way it was his best kiss!

He'd been injured, obviously, and it was *still* awesome. It was *still* the best kiss I'd ever had, which was pitiful if I really stopped to think about it. A man who kissed like that, who knew how to use his body the way Gray did, had to be pretty spectacular between the sheets as well.

Which meant he'd had a lot of practice. I was not supposed to go there but my mind could not be stopped from heading in that very steamy direction.

The thought came before I could censor it and I shook my head to try and get it away. I didn't want to consider the other women my employer had bedded. Especially not when it brought out an immediate swell of anger.

Yeah, I should try to use the word more often. *Employer*. Apparently, it was easy to forget our statuses when I looked at Gray.

The man in question was sprawled out on the sofa watching sports—of course—on the massive television. The room was dark outside the glow from the screen and the sound was barely on.

I didn't think he was actually asleep, but he could have been, for all I knew. For my part, I was pretending to read a romance on my Kindle. Pretending because my focus was not on the book at all.

Sadly, the hero on the page was not holding my attention the way Gray did. There must be something absolutely bonkers going on with me tonight. No, the problem was bigger than one night.

He just lay there, not doing anything, and yet my eyes kept shifting, checking out his body. Barefoot. The man even had nice feet. I assumed as a hockey player they'd be gross. Nope, not even *that* part of him was gross.

I sat sprawled in a large recliner across the room because I told the doctor I'd keep an eye on him. The kids were tucked into their beds, leaving the two of us alone.

I guess this is where I'm spending the night. My fingers drummed on the Kindle. Gray didn't seem inclined to move any time soon. Not that I would follow him upstairs. We'd already discussed it.

The recliner wasn't as comfortable as my bed but neither of us thought my staying overnight in his bedroom sent the kids a good message, even if he was injured. Thus, we decided on the living room and the equally massive sectional sofa there.

My hockey rink clothing had been switched out for a t-shirt and leggings. I'd rather be braless but I wasn't because, well, Gray was there. Normally I slept naked; another thing I would *not* be doing on the living room recliner. Instead, I wore a bandeau bra under my t-shirt. About as close to comfort as I'd get tonight.

"You're not *my* nanny," he'd reminded me earlier when I'd brought him some water.

If I wasn't mistaken, he'd let his fingers linger longer than necessary when he took the water bottle from me. He was trying to say I didn't have to do these kinds of things for him; it wasn't part of my job. Still, there was an implication there, something...more.

He finally broke the quiet with a question, his deep voice almost startling me out of my thoughts.

"As a hockey *virgin*, what did you think of your first hockey game today?"

I ignored his very particular choice of words. I was not a virgin, not even close, but I had a deep feeling Gray could teach me a thing or two about more than hockey.

"It was interesting," I answered slowly, clicking the screen into hibernation mode. "Faster than I expected but with fewer goals, I guess. I didn't exactly hate it until you nearly killed yourself."

"It wasn't me, it was McGuire who nearly killed me," he corrected as he swung his legs over the side of the sofa to sit up. "I like that you rushed to my side."

I shrugged. "The kids were scared for you."

"Only the kids?"

He patted the sofa beside him and although it wasn't the best idea, I shifted to go sit next to him. I really should maintain a healthy distance but my traitorous legs had other ideas and marched me across the room in seconds.

"*I* was scared, too," I admitted. "I thought you might not move again. I'm not used to the violence of the game."

It was not much of a concession; plenty of people at the rink would have felt the same way.

He stared at me for a long time. "It happens every now and then, but I'm tough, and these days I'm pretty cautious. Some would say too cautious, actually. You'll get used to it."

I shook my head. "Maybe not."

Then I jumped when Gray took hold of my hand.

"Sure you will." He kissed the inside of my wrist. "You're a tough girl. I can tell."

I don't feel tough. "I'm not so sure."

In fact I felt mushy and gooey from his small touch.

He kissed up my arm to the crook of my elbow without pause. It was a place I've never been kissed before and the sensation took me by surprise. I was so sensitive there, goose bumps popped out all over my body.

Gray looked up at me from this angle, his eyes searching mine for permission to continue. I should deny it, honestly, because in a world full of bad ideas this one was pretty epic.

I said nothing. He shifted to kiss me below the ear and heat pooled between my legs. Goose bumps burst to life down my entire left side.

"You are definitely tough and good and kind and I'm very sorry you were frightened today," he murmured against me.

"You should be resting," I said, my protest feeble even to my own ears.

He pulled back. "Esther, I'm going to be honest with you. You are sexy as anything and there is no way I can rest with you half naked in the room with me."

"I'm not half na—"

In a quick flash of movement, Gray yanked the t-shirt over my head, his grin wolfish.

"Now you are."

It was sexy and it was funny in a most unexpected way. I found myself laughing at the sheer audacity.

"You're laughing at my masterful maneuver, Esther. Not cool." Though his smile dropped, I heard the humor in his voice. "You have a beautiful laugh. I don't think I've heard enough of it since you moved in."

Oddly, I wasn't awkward in the least at being in front of Gray in my bandeau bra.

"Candace finds my laugh annoying, apparently," I said,

because his oldest had indeed complained that I laughed like a hyena. I had no idea if she'd ever heard a hyena laugh but it certainly stopped me in my tracks the first time she drew the comparison.

"That little..." Gray shook his head and kissed the spot beneath my right ear. "I'll talk to her again about her attitude."

"She's adjusting. It's all part of the process." I poked his chest, which of course didn't give at all. "Unlike this. *This* is definitely not part of the process and we shouldn't be doing it."

Was I making any move to stop him, though? No, absolutely not.

He leaned back slowly and I immediately missed the closeness of him. "Esther, I really like you as a person and I'm crazy attracted to you. From the minute I saw you I was blown away. I don't want to make you uncomfortable but there is a definite spark between us, and I want to see what happens when we ignite it."

The sound of the television faded into the background. My focus narrowed until there was only Gray.

"What if it all explodes?"

"What if we go for a sensuous slow burn instead?" he asked in return, his face searching mine for an answer. "Kind of like teenage-paced?"

I didn't know why I agreed to it—not that I said anything out loud—but I did agree because damn it, I wanted to kiss him again. And also because I was probably fooling myself on a number of levels. Fooling myself into believing that we were adults and if we started something, we would be able to stop it.

Slowly, I nodded. Heck, most teenagers fooled themselves on the regular. Didn't they?

For a man with a potentially mild concussion, Gray moved quickly, pouncing on me like a tiger, and suddenly I was pinned to the couch as his mouth claimed mine in a hungry kiss.

This one was nothing like the sweet, tender press to my elbow earlier, and certainly nothing like any kisses I'd gotten as a teen.

This was the kiss of a man who wanted to own a woman. One who would potentially die if he didn't have her near him, and damn if the realization didn't feel amazing to some secret, unacknowledged part of me.

He nipped at my bottom lip and I gasped, opening up to give him access. His hands fisted in my hair to hold me in place and his large body pressed against mine until we fit perfectly together. My hands were pinned, or I would definitely be running them down the firm, muscled lines of his back.

Gray had walked around the house shirtless enough times that I'd practically memorized every dip and ridge on his perfect body. Touching them would be heaven on earth. Having only ever been with musicians in the past, it would be a whole new experience, one I found I couldn't wait for.

His cock grew hard against my thigh. Those thin sweats hid nothing, and if I was not mistaken he'd gone commando. Holy Jesus. He felt *huge*. Long and massive. I wondered what it would be like to have him inside me even as his mouth moved against mine in demand.

My last boyfriend had been a selfish lover. I was so overdue for an orgasm I didn't have to give myself, it wasn't even funny, but thoughts of that asshole didn't belong in this moment.

Despite my desire, it was I who put the offer of *more* on hold. I pulled myself back to the feel of Gray's mouth moving against mine, his hands trailing down my bare arms, his fingers entwining with mine as he lifted my hands over my head.

He kissed below my ear again before tugging on the lobe with his teeth, and my whole body arched toward him.

"These stay here." He nipped the inside of each wrist as he spoke.

"Is that what the teenagers say these days?" I groaned out. Maybe they did. I wasn't sure.

"Sassy!" He bit my bottom lip then kissed me hard, his tongue plundering my mouth.

He suddenly broke away and shifted back on his haunches before wasting no time in shoving my bandeau bra up. His gaze made a bee-line and he groaned at the sight of my perky pink nipples, straining toward him the moment the cool air hit them.

Was there any sexier man on this earth? I didn't think so.

"Damn, woman. You've already made a liar out of me."

My brow wrinkled. "How so?"

"I guess I lied when I said the slow burn idea was even possible. Looking at you lying there, your perfect tits begging for me to lick and suck them, not to mention what I want to do to the rest of you... This is the kind of chemistry that can't be stopped. I'm so hard right now." He reached into his sweats to adjust himself. "I don't know what you're doing to me, woman, but I really don't want you to stop."

11

___

GRAY

I didn't want to stop myself anymore, either. I really didn't. Two weeks of us tiptoeing around the desire did nothing but make those uncontrollable parts of me all the more adamant to have her.

I couldn't have stopped myself even if I'd tried. She was there, and she was softer than I'd imagined. Tasting delicious. Those little moans in the back of her throat were nearly my undoing.

"What are you doing?" she asked as I traced a path down the side of her neck to her collarbone with my finger.

"I think you know."

My lips followed the path my finger had taken, kissing her, tasting her. My cock, already hard for wanting her, hardened even more and strained against the confines of my pants.

How could I *not* want her? I looked at her, at the way her dark eyes went wide and she nibbled on her lower lip, and the low stirring of desire became everything.

Still, I needed to know she was onboard. As she kept

reminding me: I was her boss and I certainly didn't want her to feel uncomfortable. Here, around me, anywhere.

If we did this, and I sure hoped we were doing it, we both needed to want it. We both needed to be on the same page because I wouldn't be able to bear her regret.

"Tell me what you want, Esther." I nipped at her earlobe, whispering in her ear.

"More. I want *more*."

That was all I needed to hear. It was the red flag in front of the bull, urging me on.

I leaned down and covered a nipple with my mouth, sucking it and circling my tongue around the hard bud as I pushed my fingers against her core. Holy hell. She was wet and needy for me. It was the most intoxicating thing in the world.

She arched closer, making me even harder. I let the nipple pop free before blowing across it and then taking the other one in my mouth.

"More." Her voice was husky with need.

I fucking loved it.

I pinched her nipple, tugging it between my finger and thumb, before skating my hand down her ribs to cup her sex over her clothes. I could feel the warmth through her sexy little yoga pants.

"I need you naked."

"I need *you* naked," she replied.

Who was I to tell a lady no? Or make her wait?

No more waiting, we were doing this. Now.

I peeled my body from hers and stood to yank off my t-shirt and sweat pants as she shimmied out of her yoga pants and undies and tugged off the bandeau bra over her head. One of these days I'd like to peel her out of her clothes. Later. We'd have time later.

For right now—

Condom. Shit, I didn't have a condom.

I sighed. "I don't have protection."

"I have some in the pool house. Get comfy." I stood there as she kissed me once and scurried out of the room. Esther was running butt-naked, unashamed, through my house.

I took myself in hand as I watched her go. I was rock-hard. *Get comfy*. Hell, that was asking for the impossible. I wouldn't be comfortable until I was inside her.

Which would be very soon if I had my way.

When she returned, I was sitting on the couch, knees spread, my hand still on my cock. She gave me a cheeky smile as she held up the little bit of foil. "Well, well. That's quite a welcome." She ripped open the condom, crossed the room, and then paused in front of me. Making sure she had my complete attention when she kneeled down to cover me with the condom.

I grabbed her tits in my hands and fondled them. She moaned. "I like that. A lot."

"I like *you* a lot," I countered. It was true, and although a small shock of embarrassment accompanied the statement, I meant every word. There was literally nothing I didn't like about the woman in this moment.

"Same."

Leaning in for a greedy kiss, I kept massaging her breasts without breaking the contact. Esther kept a hand on each of my shoulders as she climbed onto my lap. She rubbed her needy core against my straining cock once, twice, then lifted herself up and slid down it until I was fully seated inside her.

Oh my *God*. I lost all ability for rational thought at the feel of her. "Damn..."

Nothing compared to being fully buried inside of Esther. It was a tight fit, like heaven.

I managed to open my eyes and saw her with her head thrown back, black hair cascading along her spine.

And then she started to move.

Up and down she rode me, using her thighs to raise and lower herself, to maintain the tempo. Meanwhile I sucked, nipped, and kissed all the parts of her my mouth could reach. I felt her getting closer and closer to her climax as her muscles clenched around me.

I was trying to hold off until she came, my thumb circling her clit and urging her higher, and when she did my name fell from her lips like a sexy as fuck mantra.

"Gray. Gray. Gray." She called to me with each thrust. "Come with me?"

I didn't want to disappoint her. Never. So I let go and did just that.

OH GOD. I'd slept with Esther. And it was good, good in a way I couldn't describe. And...now what?

Yeah, now what, my subconscious echoed.

I didn't have the answers.

She stood in the kitchen the next morning, humming some tune I didn't know under her breath with her bare foot tapping along with the rhythm. The woman had adorable little toes, too, painted a beautiful bright red. Making breakfast for my kids while I lounged on the sofa trying not to think about everything we'd done together last night.

And all the things I still wanted to do to her. *With* her.

Oh Lord, there I went, cock twitching again. At least

my head wasn't bothering me. The one currently housing the brain that refused to work.

I grabbed the remote and began randomly flipping channels to try to get my mind off of my crotch. It didn't help. I wasn't paying any attention to the television or what played on there. Not really.

It was probably a mistake to sleep with her. So why couldn't I bring myself to regret it? If I thought about the situation logically, if I let my mind tick off why it was wrong to have sex with my nanny, then I managed to muster the tiniest shred of guilt. Tiny indeed.

It wasn't large enough to make a difference. It definitely wasn't large enough to stop me from wanting to do it again, no matter how badly the logical part of me beat myself up.

I said goodbye to the kids, kissing them on the tops of their heads before Esther bustled them out the front door and onto the waiting school bus.

My stomach flipped when she came to stand in the doorway, in the now quiet house, and just stared at me.

Grab her. Kiss her. Fuck her.

There went my subconscious again. I stayed where I was on the couch instead of getting up to follow through. It was safer if I kept a little bit of distance between us.

Damn if she didn't look amazing today. The slacks she wore perfectly emphasized her heart-shaped ass and the lean lines of her legs, while the shirt—yeah, the shirt told me everything I needed to know about those plump round breasts. As if I hadn't seen them bared for me last night. I kept my hands tucked beneath my legs to stop them from reaching for her.

"Hey, Gray, ah... Look—"

I shot her a slow, easy smile. "Good morning, beautiful. Have I told you how wonderful you look today?"

She blew out a sigh, a slight blush coloring the apples of her cheeks, and I wondered again how I'd managed to get so lucky. Not only in the physical sense but with a woman like her, someone I bonded with, someone who it seemed had fallen straight from heaven and into my lap.

Right where I wanted her.

"Thank you. Good morning," she repeated politely.

"The kids seemed weirdly decent this morning," I told her. "On their best behavior. None of them threw a tantrum about going to school and I didn't hear a peep about us making them ride the bus."

"I know." Esther scratched the side of her head. "I wonder what happened."

I shifted forward. "It's best not to question it. Otherwise, we'll jinx things and they'll come home ready to burn the house down."

"Look, Gray...about last night..." Esther trailed off, glancing in the opposite direction, nibbling on her lip.

I wanted to nibble on her lip.

My smile turned hot, feral. "Yes, last night." I remembered the feel of her beneath me. In vivid detail.

"I, ah, I think we should just think of that as a one-time deal," she told me then. She continued when I blinked at her, the words failing to process in my brain as I watched her wring her hands. "I mean, I work for you. And the kids. It's just that I...well...let's not complicate things."

What?

"Was it something I said? Did?" *Please don't let it be because of me.* I scooted to the edge of the sofa with my elbows on my knees. "I know I'm rusty—"

"It's not you," she interrupted quickly, though it did nothing to alleviate my sudden worries. "I'm going to be honest with you." Finally, she moved from the doorway and came to sit on the arm of the couch, glancing down at me. The same couch where we'd made love hours before.

Everything inside of me went cold. "Please do."

"I had a relationship with a colleague in the last orchestra I traveled with. It ended badly. He stayed and I left. He didn't want me. This will be the same, I know it. I will be the one who loses and..." She trailed off, shaking her head. "I want you to know I don't have any regrets. I'll cherish the memory but it has to be a one-time deal."

Esther was scared. I got it. I felt the same way. I felt the same fears like a mirror to hers. That didn't mean I was willing to give up so easily on this. "It doesn't have to be the same."

"I think it does, actually."

She'd shut down already, I saw with no small amount of regret. The tiny bit of honesty she'd shared with me had left no room for a discussion to take place and I knew no matter what I said she wouldn't hear me. Not really.

Well, shit. I finally met a woman I want more with and she cut me off at the knees. I tried not to let the disappointment show on my face. Why was it she constantly said the last thing I wanted to hear?

"If that's how you feel about things," I said at last.

Esther nodded once. "I do. We had an amazing night, I mean, I'll never look at the sectional or you again in the same way." She full-on blushed then which, distraught as I was, I still found adorable. "But it has to be one and done, it *has* to be. I can't risk getting attached to you, Gray. It's not you. Honestly."

Why could I not help but feel it *was*? I didn't like being lumped into the same box as whatever bastard she'd slept with in the orchestra. The thought of Esther with anyone else had me growling and grinding my teeth together.

I get how she feels. The realization didn't make me happy to hear the words coming from her mouth.

She patted me once on the leg before walking out of the room. We'd gone from making love to a fucking pat.

I stayed where I was, not trusting myself to move despite wanting to run after her. Part of me thought about taking her in my arms and shaking some sense into her. Convincing her to give me a shot to prove myself.

Did I want to make a fuss about a woman I didn't really know?

What if she was right, and we started down this road but things didn't work? I mean, I had kids to think about and worry over, a family and a career and a schedule. I had an entire life. So did she.

What if I moved too quickly and ended up messing things up for the both of us? Then what?

Maybe Esther was right. I drew in a breath, hating the conclusion I had no choice but to come to.

One and done. Okay. I'd have to live with it.

And damn if she didn't go outside and pick up her violin. Strains of a heartbreaking melody leaked in through the open doors.

And damn me, I had to listen to it.

12

ESTHER

Gray was out of town and gone for a week at an away game in New York, leaving me alone with the kids. For the first few days things went well. Better than I expected actually, and decent enough to have me loosening the tense set of my shoulders. Decent enough for me to let my guard down and start to really enjoy being a part of this family.

We got into a groove together where I cleaned the house during school hours and practiced my violin in between. I even began working on a few contemporary pieces a hot new experimental composer shared with me. I loved his work and his energy, and we were on the same page about how we could make music. He wanted to record with me but he didn't have the money to fund a project.

I could pull enough money together but was I willing to risk everything on this? I wasn't sure. Also I didn't know if I could go back out on stage again. Maybe the performer in me was dead. Maybe I'd used up every bit and there was nothing left.

Maybe I didn't have the guts to try and find out.

I divided the rest of the time between Candace, Georgie, and Ryan. Helping them with homework, class projects, and letting them help me cook. It was too easy for me to picture myself at the helm of this ship right alongside their dad. Co-parenting. Fitting into their lives comfortably because there wasn't an end date in sight.

Their father had been making pancakes for them, and before Gray, Sophie took on the challenge. They were all old enough to learn how to do it themselves. Candace had looked at me like I'd grown a third eye when I suggested the lesson.

By the time we were done? She knew she did a better job than her dad and decided it would be her responsibility from now on.

Yes, *relaxed* was the theme of the week.

Except I knew better than to relax my guard all the way. Any time I relaxed, that's when *he* chose to make a move. It's like he had a weird psychic connection to me because he always knew when to strike.

The kids were barely gone to school the day before Gray was scheduled to return when the cell phone in my pocket began to vibrate. One look at the screen and my stomach plummeted. I knew the number by heart and should have blocked it a long time ago.

Did I answer? Did I ignore it? The coffee I'd just sipped turned sour in my stomach and nerves prickled along my skin.

Right before the call cut off, I pressed the button. Why? Because I'm too nice for my own damn good. "Hello?"

"Hello there, Essie."

I shivered and not in a good way. *Essie.* Tyler had always called me Essie when we were alone. He knew what the name did to me. And once, yes, it made me lose myself.

Not anymore.

"What do you want?" I wrapped my free arm around my torso, purposely not saying his name.

Tyler Prescott was an ex for a reason.

His rich chuckle reached my ears in full effect even through the phone speaker. It was his *I'm so charming don't even bother to resist* laugh, but I knew better. "Do I need to want anything beyond hearing your spectacular voice?" he asked.

"Yes," I answered immediately. "With you? Yes."

He did nothing without a reason. And somehow he always knew when I was alone, too. I wondered what his endgame would be this time around. I hadn't heard from him in, what, eight months?

"It's been quite a while, Esther," Tyler was saying. "I'm calling to see if you're free to meet with me today."

"I'm working."

"Indeed, well, working implies you get a lunch break," he replied. Oh so smooth. "Meet me for lunch at Piccolo. Our old favorite Just great food and easy conversation, I promise. I'd really like to see you."

No way would this be anything resembling easy. I toyed with the idea of telling him I wasn't hungry. Or I had a previous engagement. A dentist appointment. Anything. But every excuse I came up with sounded like, well, like an excuse. Tyler had always been able to see right through me. Another one of his superpowers and one I'd tolerated then and loathed now.

Why was I too nice? I had no boundaries. "Fine," I agreed after a time, exhausted already from dealing with him. I pinched the bridge of my nose. "I have a free moment for lunch. I'll meet you there but I won't be able to stay long."

"I'll take it. See you soon. Don't keep me waiting."

I knew it was a mistake the moment I hung up and the old familiar stress lodged itself in a hard ball in the back of my throat. Why had I given in to him and his mind games? Why had I agreed to lunch? I could have just said no.

It might not be what you think, my ego tried to argue with me.

I knew better, no matter how my mind warred with itself.

I drove my pink Mini through the streets toward the old familiar place we'd once called our special spot. Special until I realized he took all his side pieces to the same restaurant, gave them the same treatment he gave me. The humiliation of that stung. The public embarrassment of everyone knowing he was using me except me. I'd been so terribly naive.

String foxes? I still wasn't sold on the nickname. Viola vixens might be better. Except my own nannies had taught me not to use disparaging language.

If anyone deserved curse words and derogatory nicknames, it was Tyler. Maybe the moniker should be about the men the women all chased, the men who took advantage of the women and not the women themselves. Because what was their crime? Being attracted to a handsome, talented man? Finding his charm irresistible? Dreaming of a better life? Every reader of romance novels was guilty under that definition.

The men should bear at least some of the responsibility. "No" was part of a man's vocabulary too, even if it did feel unnatural to actually use it.

Parking wasn't easy to find in the city unless one knew the secret spots. I managed to grab something two blocks over from the old brick building, walking to the restaurant and using the time to breathe in deep gulps of air and to gather myself and draw my armor closer.

I didn't want to think about the last time I'd been here, or the excuses Tyler had used when one of his devoted followers decided to make a scene.

Like an idiot I'd believed him. Like a bigger idiot I'd forgiven him.

This wasn't going to be an easy lunch, I knew, because it never was easy dealing with Tyler. I wasn't sure why I still danced to his tune. I really was *too* nice, I decided, if I was giving him this opportunity to hurt me again.

What did I want him to say? *I'm sorry for breaking your heart. I'm sorry for choosing someone else over you and making you feel lower than dirt after everything you did for me. I'm sorry I never appreciated you or took your needs into account.* After my night with Gray I could now add *I'm sorry I was a dud in bed* to the things he probably should apologize for.

Trouble was I didn't expect any of those words from him. An apology? From Tyler? Ha! Not bloody likely. Nor would it make a speck of difference now. I was over it. Over him.

The glass front door to Piccolo slid open on well-oiled brass hinges, the handle thick with an aged patina, and inside were the scents of expensive cocktails and perfectly seared filet mignon.

I glanced around the packed dining room—the place remained busy no matter the time of day—and landed on a familiar face.

Except it wasn't Tyler's face I saw right off the bat.

My mother stood up, wearing a simple black sheath dress, the soft waves of her hair the same color as my own. She looked like an aged Elizabeth Taylor with less diamonds and more class. And she stared down her nose at me courtesy of six-inch heels.

Standing next to her? My smiling father, and my sneaky as hell ex-boyfriend.

"Esther, my darling, it's good to see you." My mother held out her hands for me to take, while I maintained eye contact with Tyler. Glaring at him the tiniest bit I allowed myself.

There were eyes here, I reminded myself. Eyes ready to report on every move of the Richardson clan and their child prodigy.

The violin virtuoso.

"You're looking well, although your clothes are a little tight." Mom pulled at my ivory button-up, adjusting the buttons, tucking in the hem ever so discreetly. "Have you been gaining weight?"

I'd dressed demurely so as not to draw unwanted attention and now I regretted it. Dressing like the old Esther made me feel like her and I wasn't her anymore. The woman I'd become would have worn something soft and silky that highlighted her curves. Something in a bright color that made her eyes pop. She'd have worn spiky heels, not flats.

"Mother," I said neutrally. I ignored the weight comment. "How have you been?"

Here, I couldn't be myself. I couldn't be the Esther I'd worked and scraped and clawed to be, outside of this huge shadow of my past. The Esther I could be when I was with the kids, when I was with Gray.

My father held out a chair for me to sit and I did so, allowing him to push it closer to the table. Still maintaining eye contact with Tyler.

He didn't see anything wrong with the scene. Or my

reaction. How dare he blindside me like this? I knew of course this had to be about money or opportunity for Tyler. Nothing about this had anything to do with what was best for Esther. I was a commodity to these people.

What a sneaky asshole. He'd brought my parents into this purposely, thinking to maneuver me, corner me into doing whatever it was he wanted.

"I didn't realize this was going to be a family reunion," I said, staring down at the menu. "I would have dressed appropriately. Maybe we could have all worn matching t-shirts or something."

Just as I ignored the weight comment, my mother ignored my snark.

"Tyler phoned us, darling. He said he had important news he wanted to share with the three of us, and we rushed right over. You haven't been answering your calls." Mitzi Richardson settled herself in her own chair to my right while my father, Bernard, took the seat to my left.

Leaving me staring straight at Tyler.

"It's true, Mitzi." Tyler shot my mother a dazzling smile. He'd dressed in a casual navy-blue button-up showing off the carefully crafted muscles of his arms, although he had nothing on Gray. Gray had enough sheer power in his body to break the other man in half. "I have excellent news. I thought you'd all like to be privy to it before things go public. It's only a matter of time."

"Do tell, my boy, do tell." My father Bernard glanced up when a server approached to get our drink orders.

Tyler waited until our water glasses were filled before letting the bomb drop. "The orchestra wants Esther back. And so do I."

He didn't seem to notice the explosion as he let his

words settle on the table like ashes. That was my mind, officially blown and *not* in a good way.

No one from the symphony orchestra organization had contacted me. Was he lying? What game was he playing here?

Tyler wasn't finished. "She's special and unique. I've suffered without her. The orchestra has suffered without her. She was like a breath of fresh air personally and professionally. The world needs to hear her music, her gift. And I've been...*lost*...without her."

All of these things were spoken around me instead of to me. My eyes began to burn from holding them open without blinking.

"Essie, darling, come back to me," Tyler said, reaching to grasp my hand in his. I felt clammy, sick, trapped when he touched me.

I didn't believe a word of it. He didn't need me. He needed the ego boost that being with me provided.

And there was my traitorous mother, clapping her hands like this was the best news she'd heard all year. Even Bernard had a proud smile.

"What marvelous news," Mitzi stated. "Absolutely marvelous."

"No." The word escaped me before I had a chance to lasso it deep inside.

Tyler, to his credit, didn't let his expression waver. "I know this is a huge revelation, and as such it's going to take you some time to accept and process. I know you were expecting the symphony to refuse to accept you back after leaving on such terrible terms."

I had made a scene, hadn't I? I'd made a very public scene, and Richardsons did not make scenes without good reason and an end goal in mind.

My end goal? I'd just wanted *out*.

The symphony bore the blowback from my breakdown. There wasn't a moment that went by where I didn't regret how I'd acted in front of my friends and peers.

"But you deserve another chance. *We* deserve another chance," Tyler insisted.

Water under the bridge, and I didn't *have* to stay here and listen to Tyler's lies anymore.

I pushed away from the table. I didn't care what more he had to say. I'd heard enough. "No, I'm not going back to the orchestra," I said calmly. "And I'm certainly not getting back together with you. You treated me poorly. You haven't changed."

I stood up, but quicker than a flash so did Tyler. And then...oh God. Tyler was kneeling beside me with a ring box in his hand.

"Let me make it up to you, Essie. Marry me."

My whole body jerked as I balked, shaking my head, backing away and into the nearest table, hitting it hard enough to have silverware clinking and drinks spilling, startling the occupants. Another public scene but this one couldn't be helped. I couldn't marry him. Once upon a time, yes, I'd dreamed of this exact scenario. I'd dreamed of Tyler getting serious with me and telling me all the things I'd longed to hear.

Now I was simply nauseated and felt like I might puke.

"No, I refuse," I repeated.

"Essie, my love, be reasonable." Tyler flipped open the ring box to display an ostentatious diamond ring. If it hadn't been happening to me, I'd have found it amusing. I'm sure the other diners did. "This is a winning combination. We make the perfect pair. With your prowess on the strings and my charisma, there is nothing we can't accomplish in this life. Together we can take the world by storm if you marry me."

Mitzi nodded and clasped her hands as if her fondest wish had just come true. "Marriage! Oh, Esther, this is amazing news and a wonderful match for you. You should be happy."

"Exactly," Bernard voiced his agreement. "Think hard before you say anything else."

"Take the ring," Tyler urged.

There were a lot of things the three of them thought I should do. And think. And *be*.

"Take it!"

I swallowed hard or I might have thrown up right then and there. "Absolutely not. I'm sorry if you gathered everyone here thinking a different outcome awaited you. I have no intention of getting back together with you. Ever."

I ignored my father's outraged bluster and the way my mother began to cry in keening little wails she knew would bring the attention to her.

I drew my purse over my shoulder, sparing a glare with all the rage I felt toward my ex. "Put your ring box away. It's making me sick to look at."

How dare he do this to me? How dare he corner me like this? He'd brought my parents into this little theatrical display thinking it would help corral me into submission. Too bad for Tyler. He didn't understand how terrified I was of going back to that life.

The highlight of this exchange, I supposed, was his admission that the orchestra wanted me back. I had no intention of returning but it was a clear reminder that my talent spoke for itself.

I didn't need any of them. Not anymore. I managed a phony smile and said sweetly, "I'm done."

I blew kisses to my parents, knowing if I tried to hug them they would grab me and keep me here and break down my resolve. Then I was out of the restaurant and leaving the mess of that scene behind me.

Except the next day, when I went outside to grab the newspaper from the front stoop, I saw it. I saw the whole story and every gory detail I'd been hoping and praying I'd avoid. The headline had my knees turning to water.

Violin Virtuoso Engaged to Minnesota Philharmonic Golden Boy

Oh no. Oh God, *no*, this couldn't be happening. I held the paper in shaking hands, eyes scouring over the blurry words to make out the gist of the article. There in bold print was my childhood rehashed. How I'd been discovered at the age of four for my prowess with the violin. Pushed into lessons and concerts and sold-out shows. The albums and the pride for my family.

Then my less than graceful exit from the symphony and my very public break from Tyler Prescott.

His devastation.

Our reconciliation.

Lies.

The tears were back and suddenly my eyes burned again with all the tears I'd desperately tried to keep inside. How could they write such things? And the picture! Taken right when Tyler brought out the ring box, with my parents clearly visible in all their happiness. No one seemed to care about how pale I looked in the shot. How shocked and sick and obviously unhappy.

This was a nightmare. I tucked the paper underneath my arm as though it would make the article disappear.

Not so. My luck didn't hold one bit.

Sophie had seen the article, as she texted me to say so.

And so had Gray.

It wasn't until later in the afternoon, with the kids in school, that he cornered me in the kitchen. He'd gotten back from his away game an hour ago and although I hadn't seen him come in, I'd noticed the SUV parked in the driveway.

This time it was my turn to ignore him and the confrontation I had a gut feeling was coming.

Hey, I might get lucky, I tried to tell myself, sitting at the kitchen table like it was my life raft in a stormy sea. I might have been better off in my pool house but the kids would be home any minute.

And there was Gray, storming through the door to the dining room.

He was pissed. Bright red blotches colored his face and neck, veins popping beneath his skin. He slammed the paper down on the table in front of me. Thank goodness my hands were hidden in my lap. I didn't want him to see how they trembled.

"You didn't tell me you were engaged," he growled.

Because I'm not.

I'd already fielded all kinds of texts from Sophie about it, and wondered if she'd been the one to tip Gray off to the article or if it was a terrible twist of fate that he'd found the paper I'd stuffed in the trash.

I hadn't wanted Gray to know everything about me, not like this, not through someone else's lies and definitely not through the skewed lens of the newspaper article. I didn't want him to see everything I'd escaped from, because illogical or not, what he didn't know couldn't hurt me.

Now? Now it was out there for the public to see.

"Well?" he pushed. "Don't you have anything to say to me?"

He waited for my answer.

I wanted to tell him *welcome home*. But I knew he would explode if those words left my mouth with no further explanation.

"I'm not engaged," I told him slowly, forcing myself to lift my head and meet his gaze. "You more than anyone should know that not everything you read is true."

13

GRAY

She looked up at me with those big blue eyes, telling me she was not engaged. Begging me to believe her. As far as the whole world was concerned, she was practically halfway down the aisle already. What was I supposed to think?

How did she expect me to feel about this news? Especially considering how she'd been with me less than two weeks ago.

I carefully shut away any memory of our night together.

The damn engagement story was on every news channel and I'd had the terrible pleasure of watching the headline break on my way back from the game. Seeing my nanny's face on the screen hit me in the gut like a ton of bricks.

My chest had begun to ache as the news anchor ran through the sparse details of the tale thus far.

It was nothing good. Nothing I wanted to hear. I'd stepped out of reality and into my worst nightmare faster than the blink of an eye.

I felt like an idiot and a sucker and a whole lot of other

things rolled up into one. I'd fumed the entire plane ride home. All the way through the drive back to the house, just working myself up until I felt heat at the very tips of my ears.

This was *not* how I'd seen the situation with Esther playing out. Who would? And who the hell was this guy she was supposedly engaged to? She hadn't said a peep about the man, not one word in all the time I'd known her.

Although we hadn't exactly gotten into a discussion about past relationships. But damn it, she wasn't the type of person to hop into bed with someone when she'd made promises to another man. She had decency, class. Morals. Principles.

Or maybe I'd simply deluded myself due to wanting her so badly.

I'd slammed the truck to a stop in the garage, practically crashing through the door into the house. Seeing red when I barreled into the kitchen and found Esther seated at the table like it was any other day.

"Explain," I growled through gritted teeth.

I knew I was behaving like a beast and she even looked at me with a touch of fear in her gaze for a long minute. Too long. The shock of her expression took me down a notch and I physically stepped away from the table.

I would never hurt her or any other woman and I didn't like to see her cowering. However I was having a very hard time keeping my emotions in check.

Get a grip on yourself, Gray.

I almost managed it until I glanced down and saw the newspaper headline once again. It had me seeing red all over again. Esther was engaged to some *ponce* from the orchestra and I was angry as hell for a number of reasons. Punching a wall wasn't outside the realm of possibility.

Number one, I did *not* sleep with other men's women. I may have slept around with the odd puck bunny, and Mira of course, since Rachel passed away but not with anyone in another relationship.

I was not that guy. Not by a long shot.

Number two, *that* putz? Seriously? I'd made the connection while driving, the name finally clicking into place. I didn't have the pleasure of a personal acquaintance with Tyler Prescott and I didn't need to. I knew his look and I knew the type.

I knew his reputation.

I didn't understand much about the music industry, though as high-profile athletes we often went to galas and fundraisers where we mingled with people from Esther's old world and Tyler's reputation preceded him. I vaguely recalled him hitting on Tori once and her shutting him down fast. It seemed as soon as the name clicked home, the memories of him flooded me until I had a hard time shutting them off.

Why had Esther ever let the little weasel anywhere *near* her? How could she let him touch her, love her, share her bed? And now the world thought they were engaged.

Number three was totally on me: Why didn't I know I had one of the country's best classical musicians as my nanny?

Well, that one was easy—because I was lazy and arrogant, as my sister had been more than happy to point out. Esther had told me she'd played professionally and walked away, that very first day I saw her playing in the pool house. The woman hadn't lied. I simply hadn't bothered with any follow-up questions.

I had let my sister hire her for the position and hadn't even taken the time to read the woman's resume before letting her into my home, my family, and of course my bed. I'd assumed anyone would feel lucky to work for me and I didn't do my due diligence.

Now I paid the price for my arrogance.

The moment the news broke on the television, I'd called Sophie to ask her about Esther's past, and got a true butt-chewing from her.

"Are you serious? She has previous nanny experience, amazing references, and she's awesome with your kids. She was also a violin virtuoso with the symphony orchestra. It was all right there on her resume, Gray. If you didn't read it, that's on you." Sophie hadn't stopped there. She'd continued with the tirade for another ten minutes and I had to wonder if she was upset about the engagement news as well. "Esther's character isn't in question. You know how the media can be. Make sure it's legit before passing judgment."

If Esther *was* actually engaged, then she wasn't about to stay long on the job because I knew I wouldn't be able to keep looking at her beautiful face knowing she was destined for someone else. If she didn't leave, I'd have to make her go. Even if I had to fire her.

Which certainly wouldn't be good for my kids. I looked up from the newspaper on the table and met her gaze. And in that instant I wanted this whole thing to be just a big misunderstanding.

"You can't believe everything you read, Gray," Esther reiterated, and I knew she was right. "You should know." I did. I'd had my fair share of misquotes, statements or photos taken out of context, outright lies. It came with the territory.

I still didn't quite believe her, though. Some part of this tale had the ring of truth in it. I just didn't know which part.

"The whole freaking world thinks you and Tyler *are* engaged." I said his name like it was contagious.

I remembered the time he'd hit on Tori, and I'd looked the guy up online. Did a little digging. There were plenty of articles lauding him for his musical abilities. There were also quite a few about his personal life and his hound-dog tendencies. He'd slept his way around several orchestras through the years. He also apparently had a penchant for getting a little too cozy with his fans.

The more I'd scrolled through, the sicker I'd felt. It was only when Tori assured me there was not a chance in hell of anything between them did I finally give it up. Now it returned in full force, as familiar as an old bone pulled out to gnaw on again.

Esther jutted her chin in my direction, a little defiantly. "I don't really care what the rest of the world thinks. It's all lies and I have my lawyers working on contacting the relevant publications and news sources and demanding retractions. Trust me, Gray, if I were engaged, I would have been forthcoming with the information. You would have been the first to know. Well, maybe the second."

Her attempt at humor missed the mark with me. "To be honest?" I raked my hand through my hair. "I'm too mad to think straight right now." Better to go with the truth in the long run. Surely, I looked like a hot wreck at the moment. She must see I was on edge.

Esther didn't look happy either. A little pale, a little shaky. Did I believe her?

Did I have a choice?

She pushed her chair back from the table, letting it scrape across the floor. "Gee, you're *mad*, Puck Daddy? Imagine how *I* feel. My deplorable ex told the world we're engaged and leaked it to the news after ambushing me with a lunch he'd, unbeknownst to me, invited my parents to attend as well. I can totally see how this is all about you." She glared at me. "You know what? Believe me or don't believe me. I don't particularly care right now."

Esther had gone from contrite to furious and I kind of liked the fire in her eyes right then. Was I that fucked up?

"I'm going to my room to deal with this shit show on my own until your children get home," she finished. "Then you can rest assured I'll be the consummate professional while I handle this in my own way."

With her statement hanging in the air between us, she turned and stalked away from me. I wanted to grab her wrist and haul her against me and kiss the stuffing out of her...but I didn't.

I watched her go, with narrowed eyes and feeling as if steam still leaked from my ears. Adrenaline aftermath still fired my blood.

What if I was being played? What if she really was engaged and just wanted to get a rise out of me? Though what her game would have been, I had no idea.

I ran a hand through my hair. I'd genuinely believed she didn't know who I was or anything about hockey when she came here. Why sleep with me, *use* me, if she was engaged?

Esther stalked across the lawn toward the pool house and closed the door behind her. I could almost imagine the sound of the lock flicking. She definitely didn't want me to follow her, although I think we both knew I could break down the door if I really wanted to do it.

I'd only left the guys a short while ago at the private air strip but I stormed out of my home and headed to Dominik's place. I would normally have gone to Lucky's, but I had a terrible sneaking suspicion he was currently having sex with my sister and I'd walked in unannounced on that disaster before.

In my current state? No way would I survive the horror a second time without losing what was left of my sanity.

Naturally, when I stormed through his front door without knocking, Dom had the TV blaring and Esther's story was there for me to see *again*.

I let my head tip back on a near scream. "Turn that shit off," I told him as I stalked forward. "I can't stand to see it."

"Did you know about this?" Dominik asked, cocking a thumb toward the TV from where he stood leaning against his kitchen island. "Man, the shit they spew on the news these days. Oh poor, sexy Esther."

Thankfully he clicked off the power button and the room fell silent in an instant.

"Would I have *slept* with her if I'd known?" I growled, going to his fridge, helping myself to his beer even though it was not even close to beer o'clock.

Didn't matter. I needed something to take the edge off before I ran my entire *body* through a wall.

"You slept with her? Christ, Gray, are you serious right now? Did you have any idea she was engaged to someone else? Or is this another propaganda moment?"

I could tell Dom desperately wanted to know how and why I'd kept this secret from him.

I gulped half of the beer before I was able to speak. Wiping the back of my arm over my mouth, I told Dom about Esther and me, about our moment of weakness before the team had gone away to play New York.

He stood still through the conversation with only a few comments interjected here and there, his arms over his massive chest and his gaze dark. Mostly he was very happy for me, and maybe a little jealous. Of course he was jealous. Esther was a beautiful woman. A great catch.

Dominik didn't think it was a bad idea to sleep with her...barring what she said about the engagement being false was the truth.

"What's the problem, really?" he asked. "I don't see a problem *anywhere*. I mean, unless the story is true and she's really engaged to that other guy, but let's be honest with ourselves here. When are they ever absolutely confident about what they report? If Esther says they're wrong, they're wrong."

I shook my head. "It doesn't matter. We are not continuing with the sex—which was already decided *before* this debacle, precisely because it could get complicated."

"I think you are a little beyond complicated now." Dominik smartly kept any attempt at humor to himself. I wasn't able to take a joke at the moment.

I swore him to secrecy because it was clear Esther hadn't wanted anyone to know about the two of us. Especially not since she'd taken care to warn me several times about how it was a one and done deal. Now I questioned the motive behind her warning.

Maybe it wasn't about the job and her being under my employ. Maybe it had been about the fiancé all long.

Well, shit!

I crushed the beer can in my hand.

"You slept with a musician, and she is so far out of your league, it isn't funny. No wonder she went back to Tyler. She got tired of scraping the bottom of the barrel with you." Dominik gave me his signature smile. It might work on the ladies but not on me.

I growled again. I felt like an animal. May as well sound like one. "Do you think I'm in the mood for your humor?

She says it's not true. That she's not engaged to the dick-wad. What do I know?"

Could I trust her? Should I trust her? Did I have a reason not to? My mind went back and forth on the issue purely to torture me.

"She's got to be pissed that the tool told the press otherwise. Why would he pull this kind of stunt?" Dominik questioned, back to being serious.

He motioned toward the fridge, indicating more beer available, but I shook my head. Shrugging, he grabbed one for himself, popped it open.

Dom took a healthy swig and mused, "He probably spilled it everywhere because he wanted Esther for himself."

I wanted to say would *you* let Esther get away? Only a fool would let a woman of her caliber slip through their fingers.

But I didn't say a word because I didn't want Dominik thinking about her in those terms, and because...well, I may have just behaved like a possessive boyfriend, and a fairly aggressive one at that, instead of Mr. Casual which was who I was supposed to be. Even if she was not engaged, I didn't have the right to scream in her face.

Maybe instead of interrogating her, I should take a hard look at the man in the mirror and decide where this anxiety was coming from.

In short, though, I'd already let her get away from me. My bad mood and jumping to conclusions had pushed her right out the door.

"I'm sure Esther isn't too happy about the story either way," Dom added after taking another sip.

"Yes, she is most definitely pissed about it." I left out the bit about her being pissed at *me*, too.

Suddenly Alexi walked through the arch into the kitchen then, tipping his head in my direction in greeting. I didn't mind his arrival. Dom must have messaged him at some point.

This was the good and the bad of us all living close by. We walked in on each other often.

"Your nanny is way overqualified," he told me with a grunt.

Alexi had his baby boy Adam with him, riding on the big guy's shoulders. The kid gave me a gummy grin that had me smiling despite myself. Alexi's own nanny, Mrs. Armstrong, was very much of the middle-aged-sweet-lady variety I should have hired myself. The same type of woman I'd expected before I saw Esther on the other side of my door.

Lucky bastard.

"What do you mean?" I burst out. Ready to get myself worked up again.

"I've just been looking her up on the internet since I saw the news. Violin child prodigy is what most of the articles tend to call her. Why is she working for *you*, again?"

I might have taken offense at the joke except I realized Alexi was not joking.

"Good question," Dom agreed, pulling out his own cell phone to look Esther up. "Oh wow, she *was* a child prodigy. A virtuoso. Have you seen some of these clips? She's amazing!" He pressed play on one of the videos and the soulful sound of strings filled the otherwise quiet kitchen. "The media says her career was still promising and on the rise but she just walked away a year ago," Dominik finished.

Jesus.

"Carnegie Hall at age five. Juilliard. Gray, she's next-level talented. This is like one of us quitting at her age. Who does that?" Alexi asked, and I didn't really know the answer beyond what she'd told me about wanting to be creative and play different music.

I kept that to myself, feeling like it would be a bad idea to air something she'd told me in private.

"I don't know," I said instead.

Being around my friends had a calming effect, thankfully. I wasn't sure I'd survive the rest of the afternoon all keyed up.

"*Why* is probably a better question," Alexi offered from the floor where his son rode him like a pony.

I stifled a chuckle. Everyone thought the guy was so serious, but not with his kids he wasn't. However, he was wise and made a good point. I definitely wasn't thinking clearly enough to figure this puzzle out.

Why had Esther really walked away? There had to be more to it. Hadn't she said it was a long story? I hadn't been able to listen to her, being...*distracted*...at the time.

"Probably had something to do with this fake fiancé and his bullshit." Dom sounded certain.

"How do you know he's a fake?" Alexi said between neighs.

Dom shrugged. "That's what Esther told Gray."

I glanced over at Dominik, wondering why he felt the need to be such a know-it-all. But yes, she had told me. And it seemed that Dom trusted her implicitly. I'd slept with the woman. Why couldn't *I* trust her the same way?

Because I was hurt, and pain and fear made people react from the worst sides of them instead of the best.

At once my shirt was way too tight and choking me. I reached up to tug at the neckline, trying to give myself some more breathing room. It didn't work.

"So what are you doing here, Gray? You know what it's

like when the media is all up in your business. Esther needs your support more than ever. You guys are friends, right?" Alexi asked me. "A little more than friends, I'd wager."

He winked at me and I might have strangled him were it not for his adorable son on his back. Cheeky asshole.

Still, he made a good point about having the media up in our business. We had all been there in the past and we personally knew what a nightmare it was when they decided to shine a spotlight on your personal life.

"She's my nanny," I said, hating my lame ass as the words poured out. "I mean...I'm not even sure she wants me there for her in that kind of way."

"If Mrs. Armstrong was in this kind of situation, then I would be helping her out," Alexi said with a pointed stare.

One could only guess what he thought of me in the moment. Alexi wasn't exactly Mister Chatty; his face usually did the speaking for him. Unfortunately for me, today he wasn't giving anything away. He made sure to keep his face a blank mask so I'd search for the answers.

"That would be fascinating. I think Barry, the dude with the Doberman from around the corner on Pine Street has a bit of a *thing* for Mrs. A. I've seen them at the park, but it probably wouldn't make the news beyond the borders of our little housing community," Dom added unhelpfully before pointing at me. "However, in *your* case, you are definitely in the wrong house right now."

"Is that your professional opinion?" I asked dryly.

"Yes, absolutely. And I'm asking you to listen to me now. Go and give the woman some moral support at the very least, if not access to your expensive legal team. If she needs some PR help then I bet Tori would help her out."

"Tori works for the Raiders," Alexi barked, glaring up at

Dom from his crouched position on the floor. "She's not for outside hire."

Adam gurgled along with his father.

I fought the urge to roll my eyes at the man's drastic change in demeanor. He was not a fan of Tori, which I didn't understand at all. Tori was cool and she and Sophie were tight. I shuddered to think what kind of secrets those two liked to blab to each other about.

Nothing good, surely.

"She's one of us, dude, as is Esther. Tori would help," Dominik insisted. He finished his beer and set the empty can on the countertop for recycling. "She'd probably be super stoked to help because she's a legitimately nice person and a damn good PR rep."

Dom was like that himself. He would help anyone. The man was still friends with his ex-wife, for goodness sake.

Out of everyone on the team, Dominik might look the most intimidating—only a step behind Alexi—but he had a heart of gold and was the one who went out of his way to do nice things for others.

And in this case, I had to agree. Tori probably would help if I asked her. She was the PR manager for the Raiders, but she was also the daughter of our billionaire owner. She and Esther probably had loads in common, having both come from money. Old money. Not like me and the guys. We'd worked our way up the ladder after starting from the bottom.

"And if you don't get your ass home to Esther," Dominik was saying, "then I'm going in your stead. Maybe she and I could find some things to talk about."

He said it to get a rise out of me. I knew it. He knew it. Even so—

Hell no! I slammed my empty beer can down and

headed out as the two of them yelled out in unison, "Be nice!"

Yeah, right.

I didn't feel nice, I thought as I stalked down the sidewalk. I felt confused. I was still furious...but maybe not at Esther anymore. I was *definitely* pissed off at her jerk of an ex for putting her in this position, and I was mad at myself for storming off and not believing her.

Let's not forget sleeping with her without doing a background check.

I thanked my subconscious for the reminder. Seemed I had a lot to answer for when I finally got around to it.

Still, when I thought back on the conversations Esther and I had about her past, this latest revelation fit in with what little she'd told me. I'd heard her play, for heaven's sake. I knew how good she was and she was no amateur.

She had told me she'd walked away from her music.

No one who left a huge career like Esther's did so easily or without regrets. Strings were still attached, even if they were invisible.

My footsteps echoed along the cement as I walked, the day beautiful and the sky clear overhead. It wasn't the type of day to be this angry.

I supposed everyone's reasons for doing things were different, but I did know this: anyone who quit like she did? They shunned the limelight. That was true if nothing else.

Which meant she must be *hating* this media circus. And what had I done?

Acted like an asshole, of course.

I let myself in the front and called out for my family. Shouldn't the kids be running to the door to greet their dear old dad after his away games? They were out of school by this point. I followed the sound of raised voices and found

Esther lying on her stomach on the living room floor, surrounded by a pile of cushions, with my kids scattered around her listening to her read out loud. Georgie had her head in her hands, her legs dancing back and forth behind her. Even Ryan was sitting still.

I stopped in the doorway, just watching. Listening. They all looked really happy. And there I was still fuming. I didn't want to ruin this for them.

Well, shit. Esther was right.

We shouldn't be together.

And what did it matter to me if she was engaged? My kids would always come first.

It did matter to my heart, though. That treacherous organ beat harder just looking at her. But—and it was a big but—the kids were more important. I had priorities. I had a family to focus on and she had a life of her own, one I was not privy to.

Candace was the first one to spot me. "Hey, it's Dad!"

When they all finally glanced over, they did get up and run to me. Esther got to a seated position but stayed sitting where she was for a minute or two, watching the scene unfold, the book open on her lap.

Then she closed the book, set it aside, and rose to her feet. "Guys, I'm going to start dinner. You can all come to the kitchen in thirty minutes. The food will be ready then," she said before leaving me alone with my kids.

I knew I'd messed up in an instant.

She left, and I watched her spectacular ass go farther and farther away from me. I would not be tapping that anymore. Kids and common sense first. End of discussion.

14

ESTHER

Over dinner, Gray mouthed the words no one *ever* wants to hear. *We need to talk.*

I was trying to enjoy the spaghetti and meatballs I'd made, *trying* being the most important word, but honestly I couldn't taste anything. I was so wound up my fingers shook holding the fork and I'd stabbed myself in the lip twice now.

Still, as this was my job, I slapped a smile on my face and talked to the kids about school and homework and super heroes. I talked about whatever subject came up and I did it without missing a beat.

Gray was watching me, waiting to hear my answer.

I mouthed back "later" because I knew this conversation was unavoidable but damn if I didn't need to give myself a little processing time. Time to figure out exactly what to say to him.

No doubt he wanted more information about the article and Tyler's press statements. They were answers and info which I didn't possess to give him right now, not in a way that would make a difference. My lawyers were working overtime and I'd asked for the story to be pulled from all major networks and retractions to be printed.

None of those things would make the story go away now. The horse had bolted and there was no putting the sucker back in the barn. No matter how much money I threw at this situation, there was no making it go away completely.

I was furious at Tyler and his sheer audacity. And right now, at this moment, I was also furious at Gray. He should know better. He should trust me.

Then again...

As his *nanny*, who I was engaged to was none of his business. He didn't get to be all pissy and carry on as if he were my boyfriend when he didn't hold that title. We had both agreed that's not what this situation was, but the way he had acted earlier, anyone would have thought otherwise.

What gave him the right to overreact to events in *my* life? Not a thing.

When the kids were settled in bed for the night, he came out to the pool house for our chat. Nothing could have stopped him, I knew, and so I'd been expecting him to show up as soon as humanly possible.

I'd poured myself a glass of merlot to ease the pain of this conversation. I sat casually on the couch, and I did not offer him a glass of wine. Or anything.

He noticed.

Petty, maybe, but it had been that kind of a day, and a part of me crowed in triumph when he stood waiting for the offer.

Sorry, mister, but you'd better not hold your breath.

Sophie had messaged me to say she and a friend were going out later for drinks and invited me along. I wanted this conversation over with so I could go relax with them. Normally I would have made some excuse to blow them off.

At the moment? Dealing with everything I was dealing with, and Gray on top of it? I wasn't going to refuse. Media be damned.

"You owe me an apology," I told him. "You don't get to talk to me the way you did, Gray. It's not okay."

He nodded and had the decency to look remorseful. Remorseful and sexy. I pushed the last descriptor out of my head.

"I do apologize, Esther. I'm sorry. I was worked up and I handled things very badly. I shouldn't have blown up at you the way I did."

Huh. That was easy. It almost felt *too* easy, as Tyler had never once apologized to me. Every damn thing had been turned around and made my fault. I'd expected more fighting from Gray. I'd been gearing up for an argument, I realized, forcing the tension in my arms and legs to relax.

"Well, okay...apology accepted, I guess."

His large hands were shoved in his pockets and he rocked back and forth on those huge feet. Finally, I couldn't take it anymore. He sucked the air out of the room, and although I'd wanted the balance of power skewed between us, I couldn't take the tension anymore.

"Sit. Do you want a drink?" I asked.

He finally did take a seat, at least. It didn't help me breathe any better. "I'm good, thank you. And for what it's worth...I really am sorry. I overreacted and made the situation you have going on harder for you. That said, I do have a few questions."

Sure he did. The honesty made me smile. *A few* had to be an understatement. "I'm happy to answer, if I can. Within reason."

His grin didn't quite relieve the knot in my stomach but it helped. It helped knowing he wasn't going to fight with me. Or maybe I was deluding myself. Maybe he was just waiting for the perfect moment to attack.

I took a sip of wine. I hoped I was wrong.

"Tell me, Esther. I've seen you play your violin myself, and obviously I've done a little homework on you—today—so I have to ask." He cleared his throat, tilting his head sideways to stare at me. Those eyes of his. They hid nothing. I could stare into them all day. "Why the hell are you *really* here working as my nanny? You're a good nanny, don't misunderstand, but your music..."

Gray trailed off. He wasn't wrong. I did miss the music, every day, but it had also become the key to the prison I was held in.

I stared at him for a moment longer before taking another sip to loosen my suddenly tight throat. "It's a long story," I finally replied.

"So you've said before. Luckily for me, I have time."

He leaned forward, his elbows on his knees, his handsome face staring up at me and giving me his full attention. And sadly for me, Gray's full attention was a sexy and distracting thing. I tried to focus as I stood, unable to contain my pent-up energy any longer, and paced up and down the length of the room with glass in hand.

"Your sister is coming by to take me out later." When he didn't look surprised, I had to wonder if it was his idea. "I don't have the wherewithal to get into the details with you right now. I'll at least...okay, jeez, here is the abridged version."

With a deep breath, I spilled my guts about my childhood. The more I spoke, the less painful it seemed.

I talked about the pressure and the lack of freedom. I

told him what it was like to be always performing, always in the spotlight, when I was nothing but a child. My parents were controlling and I'd never thought I could do anything but play the violin for them. All the while they as good as abandoned me in every other way.

Physically abandoned me, in some cases. I accomplished my first world tour alone with only a nanny when I was close to Georgie's age.

"They're still controlling," I added as I continued to pace. Back and forth until my legs and knees ached. "Which was part of how the engagement sort of fell into my lap. My ex was into my status as a well-known musician and my parents' status as benefactors of the arts. He made sure from the moment I joined the orchestra to keep me in his sights. To work on me and get me on his side."

Gray's expression darkened. "He sounds like an asshole."

"We can certainly agree on that. I walked away from all of it. Him, the path my parents set out for me, everything I'd accomplished on the stage...all of it, Gray. I don't want that life, and I told them the same thing more than a year ago. I made the mistake of agreeing to have lunch with him and this is what happened. I've even had my attorneys contact the media, asked the papers to print a retraction."

"Why did you go to lunch with him if you were done, Esther?" he asked, looking like he wanted to believe me but he was still not sure.

"Imagine if you walked away from hockey. Your job, your friends. You might have walked but they're all still entwined with you, a piece of you, and you might hate some bits, and you might actually miss other things..."

How did I get him to understand the parental hold? The sense of obligation? No matter what kind of relationship we'd had, terrible or otherwise, they were still my parents. Tyler Prescott was still someone I'd been close to at one point.

I'd thought I was finally getting over it, getting stronger every day. I hadn't thought a simple lunch could hurt.

"Besides, Tyler wasn't always a bad guy, at least not with me, and I hate that there's still a part of me who wanted to see what he had to say. Maybe I expected an apology, I don't know. I certainly didn't expect an ambush," I continued. I definitely hadn't expected a ring and the media circus.

Gray nodded as though it made sense. "But your *ex*?"

I had a feeling this conversation had nothing to do with me as his nanny and more to do with the fact he thought I still had a thing for Tyler and had slept with him regardless of how I claimed to feel.

The realization rocked through me like a slap.

"I understand this is a mess. You're a little mad at me, I get it, but I've been nothing but honest with you. I can't help it if my ex is trying to win me back and he's going to terrible lengths to do it. That doesn't mean I'm going. There's nothing I can do about him or his actions. I can, however, do something about *this* situation." I pointed between him and myself, then sighed. "I'm not staying where I'm not trusted, Gray, so I'll just hand in my resignation now."

That one earned me a frown as he struggled not to surge to his feet. "Let me see if I understand. You agreed to lunch with a guy you dumped a year ago and he splashed a fake engagement over the news?"

He clearly wasn't getting some crucial piece of this, and darned if he didn't still sound skeptical.

"Yes!" I insisted, almost spilling the wine on the floor.

"That's what I've been trying to tell you all afternoon. I just want to live a quiet life as a nanny while I figure things out. I told you, I left the symphony because the music, the life, no longer speaks to me. Do you get it now?"

Finally, Gray did stand, rising up and up until I was forced to crane my head to look at him.

"Okay, so we need to shut this mess down once and for all," he said. "The retraction will help but he needs to see that you're done. Really done. I mean, you *are* done, right?"

I nodded emphatically. "But I don't know how to shut it down." It was the truth. "I have lawyers working overtime on it." And I was spending money where it didn't need to be spent.

It wasn't helping matters that Tyler didn't seem to be willing to accept that I was over him, and neither did my parents. I knew them well enough to know this wasn't over by a long shot, no matter how I argued to the contrary.

Gray cocked his thumb at me as a wide smile crossed his face for the first time all day. It was the look of a man who'd just figured out how to save the world from certain destruction.

"You and I go on a date. Let's show him you've moved on. With a real man."

SOPHIE, Tori, and I sat together in a booth in the Swirled Squirrel a few hours later with the sound of laughter in the air between us.

I was on my second espresso martini, which given the day I'd had was probably a very bad idea, and I blamed it on Tori. She'd ordered the second round. The woman was elegant and very composed but a terrible influence because for some reason I wanted to listen to whatever she said.

She continued to laugh at whatever raunchy joke Sophie had just told and I stared at her over the rim of my glass. She had the willowy elegance of so many women I knew who frequented my shows and my parents' parties. Her wealth and standing were obvious from the clothes she wore and the way she spoke, but she wasn't stuck up at all. I appreciated that. More than I was willing to admit.

The bar was gorgeous, filled with old quality pieces of furniture and enough modernity to not feel stuffy. And for some reason the booths on either side of ours were empty, which meant it didn't matter that my new friends were loud. They could say whatever they wanted without me wondering who was listening.

"No media in here, don't worry," Tori had assured me when we arrived before greeting the bar staff by their names. Either she had an excellent memory or the woman was a regular.

I loved the bar and wondered why I'd never heard of it before tonight. It was a lovely blending of old-world charm and a dark intimacy—the sort of place patrons of the symphony would love. The waiters wore bowler hats and suspenders over white shirts. Whoever styled the place had an excellent eye for detail, I thought, finishing off the last of my espresso martini with a grin.

My new friends—because that's what they felt like even though I barely knew them—loved to drink and egged me on to share my story and get sloshed along with them. After a few minutes of hesitation, I found I didn't want to say no.

It had been years since I'd had a proper girls' night. Years, or rather *never*, because none of the daughters of my parents' friends would have agreed to this. They were stodgy, sticklers for tradition, and boring. Not to mention they were terrible gossip hounds. I'd spent time with them because I'd felt like I had to. Definitely not out of any true feeling of friendship.

Of course tonight, after drinks were ordered and delivered, we three discussed the day's events, including Gray's offer of a decoy date.

I wasn't sure about the idea and I needed some advice. Gray and I pretending to be together would not be hard to pull off because we had chemistry, no doubt about that. My worry was that I was playing with fire there. We'd agreed to be friends. One and done and no repeats.

Having him flirting with me and touching me for a night *in public* was going to make keeping boundaries in place so hard. Almost impossible, I told myself. I wasn't going to pretend I didn't want him, because I did, and even *pretend* would be a hard line to toe.

Then there was the issue of my parents. The message a date with Gray sent them would be loud and clear, but it might just sever the relationship forever. Was I willing to risk them as well? They were flawed and I was furious with them but they were my family. My only family.

I'd be completely alone without them.

It left a lot to think about and not a lot of time to do it. My lawyers were working double time to correct the erroneous engagement news but it wasn't fast enough.

"A date with Gray would certainly get lover boy's knickers in a twist," Sophie agreed, pulling me from my worries. She seemed to find the idea absolutely hilarious and burst into another bright peal of laughter.

"I'd rather not think about Tyler's *knickers* ever again." I made a face and shuddered, which had us all giggling. "It wasn't like the sex was anything to write home about."

Not like Sophie's brother. I kept that thought to myself.

"Cheers to you, girl!" Sophie raised her glass. "Gray is so different from Tyler. He'll hate that. I'd pay good money to see the two of them go head-to-head."

"Tyler will definitely hate being thrown over for an athlete. He's an intellectual snob as well as being the usual garden variety snob. He assumes athletes are stupid. All brawn and no brain, and therefore beneath him." He'd made his opinions painfully clear over the years.

Although he'd never seemed bothered by his own disgusting behavior with the viola vixens. I still wasn't wedded to the name but it got the point across.

"If he'd ever been beneath an athlete, he'd see things differently," Sophie quipped.

"Oh my gosh, even I can't believe you just said that, Soph," Tori replied while I blushed.

I'd been beneath her brother and she wasn't wrong. Then again, Sophie was regularly beneath Lucky, so she definitely understood.

I drained my drink to hide my embarrassment then said, "It will certainly prove a point to him. Still, I don't want to use Gray."

Well, that wasn't true. I did want to use him for sex again but I wasn't going to. Back to the blurred boundaries. My body and my heart wanted one thing and yet my head needed to stay in charge because the consequences were too great to risk.

Sophie waved a dismissive hand. Apparently, my using her brother didn't bother her one little bit. If anything, she seemed to enjoy the idea.

"He offered, didn't he? And he'll *love* it. It's like a chest-beating alpha male's dream to knock some arrogant tool messing with his woman down a peg or two. Or fifteen.

Gray has probably been dreaming of this moment since you met him. Trust me, if he offered, he means it."

"Except—and let me be crystal clear about this—*I'm not his woman.*" I gave them both a very pointed stare. It did nothing to drive my point home.

"But your douchebag ex doesn't *know* you're not Gray's woman," Tori chimed in. She made a face at me, her perfect pink lips in a conspiratorial pout. "I hate guys who think they can railroad a woman. He deserves whatever he gets and worse."

I didn't disagree with her at all. In fact, the weird part of this was I felt like I had people on my side for once. Unlike my parents, Sophie and Tori and even Gray wanted to help me be free to be myself. They saw me when I didn't have to wear the perfect mask of a polished princess. They saw messy Esther, imperfect Esther, and they were still here.

It meant something. More than they probably realized.

"I guess I just don't want to make things worse."

I did worry that maybe I was poking the beast, and the media circus around the situation would double, even triple. What if I created worse problems for myself by trying to bulldoze my way over this one?

"How can it be worse? Do you *need* Tyler or the symphony for any reason at all?" Sophie asked. She stared at me.

I had to concede I didn't.

"Your parents are already disapproving. What more can they do?" she asked.

I bit my lip. The truth was I'd spent my whole life seeking their approval and failed. Nothing I'd done had ever been enough.

What sort of people wanted their daughter to marry a cheater she wasn't in love with? Or continue with a career she found unfulfilling? Let alone both. Maybe if we'd been poor and they'd needed money...but even that wasn't an issue for the Richardsons. Sophie was right; at this point they were a lost cause.

It still hurt.

"I guess it probably can't get much worse," I said, draining the last dregs of my martini and darting my tongue out to clean the sugar off the rim.

"And it might very well get better," Tori replied with confidence. I was glad at least one of us felt that way. "It will show them you're not coming back. Most of the Raiders are good guys and having them in your corner is a good thing. With Gray doing this, if you ask them for help, you'd have the entire team lined up for you. At your disposal."

"Most of them?" I asked, because so far they'd all been good to me, but if I needed to be on the lookout, then I should know where to watch my step.

Sophie leaned closer and stage-whispered to me, "Victoria and Alexi have a love–hate thing going. No one understands it."

"I'm right here," Tori huffed before flagging down a server for round three. I didn't object on either point. I had certainly noticed that there was some history there.

"Well, I guess if we all agree this is a good thing..." I trailed off.

Tori and Sophie were nodding in hearty agreement.

I was going on a fake date with Gray to quash the false engagement rumors and finally get rid of the ex. And somehow between the third drink and practically falling out of the car back at Gray's house, I had also agreed to let Tori lend me her stylist to help me get ready for the date in question.

At that point, I wasn't thinking too clearly. I probably would have agreed to anything and been happy about it.

I didn't *actually* fall out of the car, because as I headed face-first for the gutter Gray's big arms wrapped around me just in time.

"I got you," he said before slamming the door and sending my new friends on their way with a wave.

I wrapped my arms around him and held on tight. "Aw. You're a sweetie, Puck Daddy. When you aren't being a pain in my ass."

"The great Esther Richardson brought to her knees over a few cocktails. I never thought I'd see the day." He tightened his hold on me to keep me upright. "Good thing Tori let me know you were on the way home."

"Your home," I corrected, hoping my voice didn't sound as slurred to Gray as it did to my own ears. "Not mine."

"Are you drinking because of me or the douche-canoe ex?" he asked.

"A little of this, a little of that," I said as he practically carried me into the house. At least, that's what I thought I said. I'd never really be sure.

Gray replied while kissing my temple, "Then I'll make it up to you."

I wanted to protest and tell him no kissing of any kind, but with his big warm arms wrapped around me, I couldn't quite manage it. He smelled like soap and man and it was too distracting.

"Gray..." was all I managed to mumble into his firm chest.

"Now, let's get you to bed." A look crossed his face as he stared down at me, using his foot to kick open the front door. His eyes were hooded and his pupils were dilated. It was possible on this angle he could see right down my blouse. "Alone."

Alone was the right choice but it was not the one I wanted to make right then. I wanted to make the choice where I stripped him naked and licked him like a lollipop. Luckily, only one of us felt a little daring that night.

I let him lead me to the pool house and he waited patiently while I changed into a long-t-shirt in the bathroom. I managed to brush my teeth, remove my makeup, and pull my hair in a bun without falling over or knocking anything off the bathroom vanity. Score for Esther! It was harder than I'd thought so I deserved extra points.

I walked out of the bathroom with no pants on, the hem of the shirt trailing just below my crotch.

"You usually sleep in that, honey?" Gray asked. His gaze traveled up my legs and I wished it was his large hands instead.

"Nah, I usually sleep naked." He groaned. Exactly as I wanted him to. Heat began to curl in my stomach at the look in his eyes. "I just put this on for you. Because I'm a professional and all. Drunkenness notwithstanding." I held up a finger to prove my point. Then my stomach flipped when I saw double fingers instead.

"Are you trying to kill me, woman?" His voice was low and gruff and there was no mistaking the erection in his pants. "Do you even have underwear on?"

I shook my head and collapsed back on the bed. The t-shirt *just* covered me. Just. Was I teasing him? Maybe a little.

Drunk Esther could be a little naughty, it seemed. I tucked my knees together and moved them back and forth to draw his attention.

Gray looked at me for a beat, his eyes roaming everywhere and seeing everything. I felt it between my legs and in my aching breasts. "Yep, you're definitely trying to kill me," he moaned. "On a different night, I would peel that t-shirt off of your hot-as-fuck body and do all the things I dreamed of doing for the past two weeks. Not tonight."

I pouted. I really liked the idea. "Why not tonight?"

"Because, woman, you're tipsy. And when you were sober you said this wasn't happening again." He waved a hand from his delectable body to mine and back again.

Right then, I hated sober me. She was a no-fun stick in the mud.

"What if *tipsy* me is right?" I pushed up on my elbows to see him better. "Don't you think this is a better idea?"

His eyes went dark as he licked his lips. "You have sober you and tipsy you get together for a conference tomorrow to decide. Meanwhile, there's aspirin and water beside your bed. Get some sleep. Tomorrow morning will be most unpleasant otherwise. The kids won't give a crap if you're hung over."

He stalked away toward the door. Closing the small distance at lightning speed. As if he needed to get away from me, and fast. I really hated how fast he wanted to disappear on me.

"Night, Gray," I called to his back.

He didn't turn back so I peeled my t-shirt over my head. But then I guess he did turn around because I smiled when I heard him say, "Fuck me."

Just as the shirt hit the floor.

15

GRAY

I loved the feeling, the rush of pure heart-pounding adrenaline, when we skated onto the ice as a team. There was nothing like it in the world.

All my life, I'd enjoyed being part of something bigger than myself. I loved my sister, but growing up, my best buddy was one of seven brothers and I remember being so jealous. He had a built-in team. A built-in backup system ready to go to bat for him at any time.

Lucky for me, hockey gave me the same thing.

I'd laced up my first pair of skates before I started school. My dad, bless him, was kind of a fanatic, and he played with a local league, so it was natural I'd love hockey, too. Unlike him, I didn't injure myself on the ice. With a lot of practice and hard work, I made it all the way to the NHL.

Still, on a good day, I felt the same buzz getting on the ice as I did as a kid.

Life off the ice, on the other hand, was so confusing.

There were too many gray areas and issues to navigate. I often felt like whatever I did, I screwed up. On the ice, I knew the rules, and so did everyone else. The odd asshole broke them on occasion but then there was a clear consequence for that. Penalty box. Suspension. Whatever punishment fit the crime.

Life wasn't quite so black and white.

I'd played with a few teams since I started as a Pee-wee, but there was no team like the Raiders. The players seemed to click with each other in a way I hadn't experienced before. We were a family in every sense of the word.

As the Captain of the Raiders, I led by example. I loved that.

The way the guys looked to me, the way the rookies were equal parts nervous and awe-inspired, the way the other team sometimes cowered...yeah, I was respected here. No one told me my pancakes were crap or that I couldn't kiss them.

There were no secrets on the ice.

Secrets affected the game, and no one was willing to jeopardize a potential win.

Today we were playing a team from Phoenix at home in our own arena. Ice hockey in the desert was a weird thing but this was the twenty-first century. You could get anything you wanted, anywhere. Before I signed with the Raiders, I'd nearly gone to Phoenix.

I couldn't imagine that now. Minnesota and the Raiders were my team, my family, for life. People got traded all the time in hockey but not me. I'd probably retire rather than go play for another team.

The game kicked off with a spectacular save by Dominik and heated up from there. My mind was sharp with laser-like focus, everything else blocked out.

I ran a tight ship, sure, but this was hockey and there were always fights. I watched as a Phoenix player tried to knock out one of our rookies, Mitchell Abrahams, by sliding a skate between his two legs. Big mistake, because Alexi had seen the maneuver too and he was gloves off, going head-to-head with the guy in a matter of seconds.

I didn't think Alexi even much cared for the young player he raced in to defend. That's just how it was. He defended our team, and because the Phoenix team never wanted to give up, it was three men against three in a matter of seconds.

Mayhem and madness, I thought with a shake of my head.

A mass of our purple and green and black shirts piled in with the orange and red of the other team. A violent, seething rainbow. People who didn't know hockey were often shocked by the brawling. The rest of us knew it was part of the game.

There was nothing like sitting behind the Plexiglas when a player was rammed up against it. I was close enough to the side of the rink to see Esther's wide eyed expression when Lucky did just that with a Phoenix veteran who couldn't leave well enough alone. He pressed the other man's face into the Plexiglas, with the referee blowing his whistle to try and get the fighting to stop.

I sent Esther what I hoped was a reassuring smile.

Having her there in the stands was a new feeling. Like all my feelings for the woman, it was mixed. I really liked knowing there was someone seated in the private booth who cared about me for *me*, not because of the jersey I wore.

On the other hand, I had a feeling the violence offended her genteel sensibilities, and I worried what she might think of me after today's game. This wasn't her world, not even close. She was doing her best to fit in with the gang and the culture.

I wondered if one of the things holding her back from me wasn't *this*. This life of brawls and bruises, black eyes and beat downs. Despite what people thought, and I wasn't complaining because we were highly remunerated for our efforts, hockey life was hard. There was pain and injury. There was a lot of travel, most of which involved gyms, arenas, and charter flights with very little down time. I loved my job, and yet I knew there were a lot of divorces and those stats made sense to me.

When Rachel had been sick, it was so hard to leave her. I felt like shit every time I walked out the door for an away game. She was stoic but that didn't make it any easier.

Esther, on the other hand, was used to a life of travel and upheaval, based on what I'd learned about her childhood. And yet she'd walked away from all that.

I wasn't sure what she'd think of this life or the potential of her getting thrown right back to a place she'd wanted to escape.

Huh. Why was I even wondering about that? She was my nanny. Nothing more. Even if it felt like more, it was nothing I should distract myself over.

And yeah, I'd slept with her. And sure, she'd shut me down. And yes, I was jealous when I thought she was engaged. And yep, somehow I had volunteered to go on a date with her to show her ex what was what.

It wasn't like we were *actually* dating and this was a *real* relationship.

How Esther felt about my career and hockey didn't really matter. At least it shouldn't matter, but somehow it did. I'd left the first game she'd come to with a head injury. I wondered what she thought about today's game...which I should be concentrating on. We were up 2–0 and nearing the end.

Head in the game, asshole, I reminded myself.

No one scored in the final minutes, though Lucky made a valiant attempt at a hat-trick and Dom saved a shot that looked un-save-able to me. The man was a genius in goal defense so it was still eventful. We'd managed to kick the Phoenix team's ass, and they were pretty good. Really good, actually, and we were all properly exhausted when we hit the showers.

"Are you coming to poker night on Friday?" I asked Lucky as I pulled on a dark henley shirt.

He stood naked beside me, staring into his locker like it held more than one outfit and he had to decide which one he preferred. "Why wouldn't I be?"

I shrugged. "I don't know, thought maybe you'd want to hang with your girlfriend and ditch the rest of us."

If I could get a night alone with Esther, *I'd* ditch the game. But I knew she'd be busy talking to Tori about the best way to handle the engagement retraction.

Lucky slammed his locker shut. "As you know, my name is Lucky, and lucky for me, your sister already knows that poker night is an important part of my life, so she's cool with it. Thanks for that, man."

He was right, of course. The truth was I had unfairly blamed Lucky for stealing Sophie away from me, and for the need it had created for hiring Esther. If he'd just kept his hands off my sister, then my already chaotic life would not have been upended.

"I'll see you there," I said before heading to collect my family.

I pushed out of the locker room and toward the concession stands where I'd told them to wait for me.

Esther stood there, looking adorable, talking to Tori and the kids. Unlike everyone else, who wore a jersey to today's game, she had decided to wear a purple shirt in our team color to support us.

I had offered her another jersey but of course she'd declined.

I pasted a smile on my face, and when I walked toward the group Ryan flew at me. I caught him mid-flight. "There you are!"

"Great game, Dad. You were awesome!" The kid had so much enthusiasm. I loved it, and hugged him closer. "You were great out there."

"Thanks, buddy."

"I'm glad no one hurt you this time," he said with a grin.

"Me too," Esther added. "Though how no one got seriously injured, I'll never know."

"You're not at the symphony now," I replied. And then I winked. "It's part of the action. Just like the mascots and the funnel cakes."

She pursed her pink lips. "Of those three, the funnel cakes are my favorite."

I laughed. "Tough to beat. Now, shall we go home? I'm starving."

"Well then, lucky for you there is pulled pork in the slow cooker and coleslaw in the fridge. We can feed you in five. Well, five minutes after we get in, anyway," Esther said, letting Ryan take her hand and mine to lead the two of us through the tunnel.

"Pulled pork is our favorite, Dad." Georgie took my other hand, all wide-eyed and awed tone.

"Is it, now?" I knew it was, but we never made it or came home to a house smelling even remotely that delicious. Sophie was a great auntie and nanny but not much of a cook beyond the basics. So pulled pork always came from restaurants. Esther deciding to make it from scratch was something new for us.

"It's all right," Candace muttered with a shrug, although we all knew it was her favorite, too. She wasn't willingly going to admit she liked having Esther around.

I guess I wasn't the only one conflicted about the newest addition to our household.

POKER NIGHT at Dom's was a regular thing for our team. If my house was considered the playground for the kids, then Dom's was slated for adult activities only. We could go out but we were pretty much recognized wherever we went. Autograph hunters, puck bunnies, rabid fans, they always found us.

We appreciated our fans but sometimes we just wanted to drink a beer and shoot the shit. Dominik had a cool set-up in his basement for this very reason and weekly poker nights had become routine.

I needed time with my boys. Having Esther around me looking all sexy and desirable, and me not being able to touch her was its own kind of torture. Every once in a while, escape was expected.

It was a few days after the Phoenix game, and that night she'd served me up a loaded pulled pork sandwich, all while wearing a frilly apron over her jeans. I should have been focused on the truly spectacular flavor. Instead, I remembered how *she'd* tasted and the sandwich turned to cardboard in my stomach.

I'd had several inappropriate thoughts about her doing the same thing in just the apron...and then felt like a jerk for fantasizing about her while she made my kids' dinner. Then to top it off, she brought out all the fixings for a make your own ice cream sundae bar, which we enjoyed while playing a feisty game of UNO together.

It was a great night that had even Candace looking a little bit in love with Esther.

How was I going to resist this kind of temptation?

Tonight, I needed space, because we were *not* an item and yet we were about to take our fake relationship live and in public in a couple of days, attending a charity concert featuring her former orchestra. It had been my stupid idea, of course, and now I was regretting it. Not because I didn't want to help her. But because her parents would be at the performance and I knew they had the home ground advantage. I was an outsider in their world, and as much as I was happy to be a big fuck-you to the ex and her parents, I was conscious my ineptitude could make it worse.

Bottom line: I didn't want to embarrass either of us.

I was the second to arrive at Dominik's for poker night, after Seamus. That poor man had the look of a guy who wanted to join the Single Dad Hockey Players Club something fierce. I didn't blame him, I thought as I clapped him on the back in welcome. His wife, Brittany, was not one of my favorite people. She was a gold digger and a nasty piece of work. They had two kids together whom Seamus adored and I suspected he was only with Britt these days because of them. She was with him for the lifestyle and didn't care who knew it.

I hoped the man had an ironclad prenup in place. If the misery on his face was anything to go by, he couldn't hold out much longer. He perched on a stool at Dom's wet bar, sucking back a beer. I clapped him on the back a second time. "Dude."

"Hey, Cap." Seamus tipped his bottle my way as I

placed the platter of nachos Esther had insisted I bring on the bar. He eyed them for a half second before digging in, then groaned. "Wow. Hot new nanny is a keeper if she cooks like this."

"Maybe" was all I said.

Everyone already knew about the articles and her supposed engagement. "You think she'll stick around?" he asked through his second bite.

"I hope so."

That was certainly true. The house ran better and the kids were happier with her there. The girls might have been slow to open up but I saw how they were coming around.

She brought order and she also brought joy, something we'd been lacking even with Sophie there. We'd been stuck in a rut since Rachel died, spinning our wheels more or less. Esther's cheerful presence had changed everything within our four walls.

"You tapping that?" Seamus asked casually. "And if not, why not?"

I glared at him. "She's my nanny, man. We don't talk about her like that." I sounded mad and I was. I didn't want anyone thinking about *tapping* Esther but me.

"Sorry. I'm living vicariously these days." He sighed, taking a laden tortilla chip and shoving it in his mouth as I thought about what to say to stop him from going on.

"He's taking Esther on a fake date to freak out her ex," Dom said to Seamus, walking over to join us with a wide, mischievous grin. "Well, if he can remember it's fake."

"I can effing remember, thank you!" Wow, I needed to calm down. I knew I was jumping down the man's throat and I couldn't seem to make myself care. "I'm helping out a friend who needs help," I said slowly. "Nothing more."

Dom's smile went wider, hotter. "Of course you are."

I didn't like his condescending tone. Before I could say anything else, a few more of the guys showed up and it was time to play poker.

It was like an explosion of sound and energy. Apart from Lucky, Dom, Seamus, Alexi, and myself, we were joined by four other team mates. Our usuals. Mitchell Abrahams, Liam Montecino, Wayne Havel, and David Costanzo drove over together.

They were a good bunch, and I hoped we could settle in and play some poker without the conversation returning to Esther.

That was apparently too much to hope for.

"Why wasn't your girl wearing your jersey at the game, Puck Daddy?" Mitch the rookie asked me.

I took my place across the table from him while Dom began to shuffle the cards. "She's not *my* girl, for the hundredth time. She's the kids' nanny. And a *friend*."

I made sure to drive the point home.

"Yes, but if you want to convince her family it's more than that, she has to *look* like your girl," Alexi said with his habitual scowl. He watched every move Dominik made as he shuffled.

"And wear your jersey," Mitch felt obliged to add.

"I feel confident in saying her folks weren't watching the game," I retorted, looking down at the crappy hand of cards I'd just been dealt.

Maybe I should have been watching Dom shuffle too. He must have kept the good cards for himself. Or maybe I just had shitty luck right off the bat.

Seamus shrugged. "You never know."

"Based on what Esther has said, I'd be willing to bet I'm right. I'm not betting on these cards, though." I set them down on the table. "I fold."

As the game went on around me, the guys felt obliged to tell me all the ways Esther and I could sell this relationship and kill the engagement rumors. Unfortunately, almost all of them involved being way too close to Esther.

"You could make a sex tape," Mitchell stupidly offered as a suggestion.

Alexi rightly gave him a slap to the back of his thick head. That one had a lot to learn, on and off the ice.

"Or just let the media catch you making out somewhere," Dom advised, laughing. He set three chips down. "Take her for a meal somewhere, like as a pre-date."

I knew I hadn't been in the dating game for a while but I had no idea what a pre-date was or if that was just some bull Dom had made up.

"No pre-date. Just one night at the symphony," I said as I got up for more beers. I didn't want to hear anything else and knew the guys would not be able to shut up.

"You don't think she'd be fun to date? I should have volunteered for the job of her fake boyfriend. I would have fake-dated the life out of her. She'd have loved fake-dating me so much she'd have been ruined for other men."

I whipped around, ready to pounce. Dom apparently had a death wish, and I wasn't in the mood to stop myself from obliging him. In two steps I was across the room and had hauled him out of his seat with one hand, lifting him by the collar of his shirt. "*Stay away from her, man.*"

The rest of the guys went wide-eyed and silent. Dominik just smiled and spoke again, this time the sarcasm evident. "Yep, it's completely platonic with Esther, and you have no feelings for her at all. I see."

I dropped him like a hot potato. He'd played me, the bastard. For a long time, we stood watching each other.

"I didn't come here for this shit," I finally barked.

"No, you came here to get away from the hot nanny who you have feelings for, who you're about to fake-date," Alexi stated, groaning. "Now, can we please play poker? That's why *I* came here."

The rest of the game passed completely uneventful. There were no further outbursts, and although I lost a little bit of money to Lucky, of all people, I actually had fun. Dom had played his part to perfection and ended up winning the whole jackpot.

He was still a bastard. Unfortunately, he was a bastard who had proven his point. I shouldn't have given him the reaction he wanted.

When I stumbled home, Esther was in the kitchen. Her laptop was the only light in the room and illuminated her face with a soft glow. She wore a white tank top over a pair of leggings, with her dark hair piled on top of her head.

She glanced up at me standing in the doorway and smiled. It was a smile that took my breath away. She was beautiful, no doubt about it, but she also radiated it from the inside, all sweetness and goodness.

"Did you win?" she asked softly.

"It's not really about winning."

"I'll take that as a no." She tilted her head. "You're a highly competitive guy. If you'd won, you'd be crowing about it. Guaranteed."

I liked how she was teasing me. "Oh really? You think you know me so well?"

I didn't want any weirdness between us. Teasing meant she'd forgiven me for being an ass to her when the media leaked the engagement story.

"Can you get to be the captain of an NHL hockey team without being competitive, Gray?"

I scoffed. "Doubtful."

"Then that's all I need to know." She smiled again as if she was relishing her own verbal victory. She was more than a little competitive herself, I'd come to see. "The kids all went off to bed easily tonight. Even Candace was remarkably compliant. I hope she's not getting sick. Think it might be a return of their stomach bug?"

I stepped closer and mirrored her pose leaning across the island. At least I couldn't touch her from here. "Maybe she's starting to accept you," I said.

"Seems like a more positive scenario, doesn't it?" Esther bit her lip, and then glanced down at her laptop instead of looking at me. "Are you, ah, nervous about our date?"

I decided to go with complete honesty. "A little. You?"

She nodded. "I'm thinking maybe it's a bad idea."

That earned her a laugh. "No maybe about it, honey. It's definitely a bad idea but it's all we have. He'll get the message loud and clear, without question, then you won't have to bother with a fancy team of lawyers to keep him away."

"Do you promise to keep your hands to yourself?"

"I promise not to touch Tyler," I told her. Pushing up to a standing position. "I can't make the same promise about you."

She let out a small gasp and I saw her nipples pebble beneath her thin tank top. Mmm, good. A perfect reaction, one I was glad not to miss.

So...I wasn't the only one who felt more than a little conflicted. We'd just have to wait and see who caved first.

16

GRAY

I knew at once. This was a very bad idea. Very bad.

Why had I let myself get carried away with the whole idea of proving something? I didn't need to prove anything to anyone. And yet somehow I wanted a *big* act to shut up her parents. Her bastard ex. I wanted to do something to lay claim to her and show them Esther wasn't just an asset to flaunt around for their own purposes.

She was a human being with a bright and beautiful soul and a smile to match. How did they not see those things in her? How could they want her to be with someone like Tyler?

I didn't understand a bit of how their minds worked and honestly I didn't want to.

So, where were we tonight? Oh yeah. We were going to see the Symphony Orchestra perform for a black tie gala charity event.

Yes, *very* bad idea.

Her ex would be there and I knew how hard it was gonna be for me to keep from punching the guy straight in the nose. Okay, despite the roughneck quality of professional hockey I'd never been the fighting type. For Esther's dignity? I might discover some hidden alpha male energy. I might react poorly. In public, no less.

I also didn't know my ass from my elbow when it came to classical music. Luckily I did own a tuxedo; even if it smelled slightly of moth balls, it still fit well enough I didn't feel like an organ grinder's monkey in it. And the gown Esther wore tonight...my mouth went dry at the sight of her. The floor-length gown she wore was out of this world insane. Silk, black, and backless, apart from a sleek silver chain dangling along her spine.

I knew Tori'd had a hand in that outfit and I didn't know whether to praise her or curse her. I was going to be rock-hard all damn night.

Esther Richardson was the most gorgeous woman in the concert hall. Hell, the whole damn state of Minnesota, and I dared anyone to change my mind.

She wore a single strand of pearls perched just along her collarbone and drawing emphasis to the area. She didn't need any other jewels. The whole of her shone, from her curling hair to the tips of heeled shoes adding length to those long lean legs. Her makeup was minimal and artfully done, from the lips to the liner around her eyes.

This was Esther the debutante and socialite. Not Esther my nanny, who babysat my kids and cleaned up their barf.

I found I liked both.

The moment we walked through the revolving glass doors into the concert hall, eyes turned in our direction. Cameras snapped and flashes went off with a jumble of voices calling out to both of us. On a normal day, I was used to the attention. I'd been through all this and more during my years with the Raiders.

If I was just some man candy accompanying the famous

Esther Richardson, this would be bad. But I was the captain of the Minnesota Raiders, and the buzz was real. Real—and something we'd have to try and weather together tonight.

"Which one of us is the bigger deal?" she leaned close to ask me. We pushed our way through the crowd and she offered them a small, polite grin.

"Oh, probably me," I teased as I waved to the crowd. "Or the fact that I'm here. With you. Together, though, we're a *huge* deal."

The compliment didn't go as well as I'd planned, if the way her fingers tightened on my arm gave me any clue. Apparently, Esther didn't like the limelight anymore.

"It's because you look dazzling tonight, Esther." It was my attempt to salvage her nerves.

She sighed. "If we're going through with this, then I need a little liquid courage. I'm not sure I'll be able to face my parents or deal with the rest of it without a slight buzz." She gestured her nose in the direction of a bartender with a cascading fountain of champagne and glittering flutes ready to be filled.

"Oh, you little lush. Please. Lead the way."

She'd certainly been sloshed when the car Tori had hired to drive them around dropped Esther off at home last night. I said *home* because I didn't care how badly she argued with me about it, it was her home as much as mine now, no matter that her name was not actually on the deed.

She might not have been in full possession of her wits last night, but even so, the woman knew how to tease me. The sleep shirt bit had been almost too much to bear. It had taken me precious minutes of standing outside her door doing deep breathing exercises to keep from going back inside and fucking her until she screamed my name.

A delightful fantasy. One I made sure to keep in my

head and not turn into reality because I wouldn't take advantage of a drunk woman.

"Gray? Come on."

She tugged me toward the display and we grabbed two of the flutes, the liquid inside fizzing happily. I might need a little liquid courage too. A hell of a lot more, I thought as a sour-faced couple approached us.

"Here they are," Esther whispered from the corner of her mouth. "Get ready for the ride of your life."

"I'm ready."

Yeah, I wasn't ready at all but this *had* been my idea. Esther introduced the two of them as her parents.

"Mitzi and Bernard Richardson, meet Gray Wright. My friend and employer."

I would have liked her to tack on *and most amazing lover of my life* to the descriptors but I'd take what I could get.

Plastering a large smile on my face, I held out my hand for a round of introductions, towering over the couple. "It's a pleasure," I said.

Except it clearly wasn't a pleasure for them. If looks could kill, then I would be a corpse. Bernard stared up at me as though Esther had lifted a rock from the garden and found me slithering underneath it. Mitzi's gaze lingered a bit too long on the tight fit of my tuxedo jacket before her nose raised in a slight sniff.

Musclehead. I swore I almost heard her say the word bouncing around her brain.

Hell, I'd thought I looked pretty good tonight. Even with my millions in the bank, it wasn't enough for these people because I wasn't old money. A *nouveau riche* joke. And an athlete to boot.

Esther simply looped her arm through mine and kept

her same placid, sweet grin in place in a way I knew I would never be able to match.

Maybe I needed a little more practice.

"What is it you do again, Mr. Wright?" Bernard asked me as he feigned interest in my answer.

Mitzi nodded along with his question as if she too was vastly interested. As if Esther had never mentioned my profession, I thought dryly.

"I'm a professional hockey player with the NHL," I told them. "I play for the Minnesota Raiders."

"NHL," Mitzi repeated, emphasizing each letter. "What does that mean, exactly?"

She snapped her fingers to the attendant and instantly two full flutes were handed over to her and Bernard. From the look on her face at the first taste, the quality of the bubbly wasn't up to her standards.

I'd thought it tasted pretty good.

"It's the National Hockey League," Esther answered smoothly for me. She took a discrete sip of champagne. "Gray plays center and he is team captain for the Raiders. He is breathtaking on the ice."

She might as well have been discussing the chemical properties of dirt for all her parents cared. Bernard seemed infinitely more interesting in counting the bubbles in his glass, while Mitzi looked like she would rather be anywhere else. She stared around at the crowd and found them lacking too.

The tension popped the moment my first fan came up to me requesting an autograph.

"I'm so sorry to bother you, Mr. Wright. So sorry! But your last game against the Arizona Coyotes was absolutely amazing. Do you mind—" The slight woman gestured to her playbill with tentative hands.

My attention divided, I made my apology to the Richardsons while I took up a pen to sign.

"Absolutely fine, no worries."

Except I couldn't help but dial into the conversation Mitzi and Bernard sprang on Esther when my back was semi-turned. As though I wouldn't be able to hear them.

"*This* is what you're doing?" Mitzi hissed. "You're nannying for a man like this? You're wasting your life looking after some macho beast's children because he's too busy to raise them himself? It's absolutely beneath you."

"I completely agree, dear," Bernard stated. "How could you give up your music to pursue an avenue like *this*?"

"I don't believe I asked for your opinion—" Esther tried to cut in.

Bernard bowled over his daughter. "It's not like you need the money, Esther. You have plenty of money. There's a substantial trust fund as well. Why on earth would you choose to be a nanny, of all things? Is it to spite us?"

That took me by surprise.

Wait a minute...I'd had no idea Esther didn't need the money. My pen paused on the second round of playbills I was signing.

Why was she working at all? Clearly the Richardsons were well off; it was evident in their grooming, their clothing, their accessories, their bearing. I should have figured Esther was well off too, but...I guess I didn't really think about it. I'd been too wrapped up in *her* to think about her social status or the health of her bank account.

"Why won't you go back to the symphony?" Mitzi pushed.

"I don't belong there anymore, Mother."

"Belong? Darling, you belong nowhere else. You've been gracing the stage since you were five! Do you not understand what a waste of your talents this nannying business is? My God, you are lowering your standards!"

Being with me and my children was *lowering her standards*? My teeth ground together and a soft growl escaped.

One more word, I promised myself. One more word about my kids and I was going to let the Richardsons have it. They could insult me all they wanted but my kids were innocent, and fuck, they loved Esther. She was amazing with them.

The next person in the fandom line stepped forward for an autograph and I mechanically obliged them.

One more word and those two stuffy pricks wouldn't know what hit them.

Behind me, Bernard was telling Esther to be reasonable and reconsider her life. Her entire life, as though working for me would somehow damage whatever they'd built for her.

Neither of them gave her a chance to speak. They bowled over her until Esther fell silent and simply let the wave of their words wash over her.

Suddenly a hand fell on my arm, drawing my attention away from the growing line of fans waiting for me to sign whatever they had handy.

"Gray, it's time to go in," Esther told me, her eyes strained.

I noticed then how Mitzi and Bernard were already a few feet away from us with their backs turned. No doubt headed to their private box and done with whatever conversation they'd wanted to have with their daughter.

Aw, poo. They hadn't even said goodbye. And here I thought I'd made such a dazzling first impression on them.

"Of course, darling." I sent an apologetic glance toward the fans who would not be getting their autographs and allowed Esther to draw me in the right direction.

This was her world, I reminded myself. This was the world she'd been born into.

She didn't need the money.

How had I not seen it?

I felt like an idiot and had to juggle everything I thought I knew about her into new places.

We found our section and took a seat. It was show time —and a completely different show than the ones I was used to. A thin tremor of excitement filled the air while the orchestra tuned up on stage. The lights were low, subdued. How different from the lightning bolt through the blood excitement before a hockey game.

"I'm sorry," she began.

"For what?"

"For what my parents said about you. I know you heard everything." She stared ahead at the stage and I saw something like regret flash across her face. "They literally don't know any better. They're small-minded."

"I'm not going to take anything they say personally, don't you worry." I tried to get comfortable in the tiny seat and found it way too small. This was going to be an uncomfortable performance for a number of reasons.

We were close enough to the stage that I could make out the individual expressions on the faces of the string section. And there, leading them? A smug son of a bitch with a perfect hairdo and a very punchable chin.

His gaze flashed toward our row and beside me, Esther tensed. Her ex was staring at her when I focused again on the stage.

"Easy does it," I told her. "All part of the play."

"Part of the play," she repeated with a sigh. "Exactly."

I wanted to tell her she deserved so much better than a man like him. And I didn't need to know him personally to know his type. I watched him schmooze the rest of the ladies around him, full of himself and arrogant. I watched the way he handled his instrument—like it was his cock—in a way that let the others know exactly what he could do with it.

Okay, it *might* have been the right move after all, this public display of ours to dispel the engagement rumors. The way the ex's eyes kept darting toward Esther, I knew it was only a matter of time before I got my chance at confrontation.

She's mine.

The moment Esther at last settled beside me, I couldn't resist resting my hand on that silky thigh of hers as the performance began. After a brief moment she reached for my hand and held it in her own, squeezing every now and then as if drawing strength from me. I was happy to oblige.

With the opening chords, I knew right away nothing we heard tonight could measure up to the way Esther played her violin. To me, it was pedestrian and dull compared to the virtuosic way she performed at home. Everything inside of her showed through her music. Her passion and intensity infused each note, reaching for and drawing out sounds that literally changed everything.

She was so much more than I'd first thought. Bigger and brighter and more complex on multiple levels.

But she was also so much more than just my nanny. And that was not a little humbling.

17

ESTHER

Meeting the parents hadn't gone as poorly as I'd imagined in my head, but it hadn't been good, either.

When Gray suggested putting on a charade for them and Tyler, to pay them all back for the ambush at Piccolo, I'd thought him mad. Crazy and filled with a need for revenge. I'd preferred to let things go and sweep their behavior under the rug.

Too nice.

Yeah, I was too nice. Maybe he was right and I needed to stir the pot a little. Show everyone I was through being a doormat and they couldn't just walk all over me and get away with it.

At least Gray had stopped bringing up the newspaper articles.

I'd figured Mitzi and Bernard would both be on their best behavior considering the media presence at the symphony event. They were adherents of strict decorum in public, and as for the symphony, well...my parents never missed a concert even after I'd left it.

Yet they'd thrown more than their fair share of cutting glares at Gray simply because he didn't fit into the neat little box of their world.

Their world. Not my world. Not anymore.

They'd insulted not only me but him by association. A brute, they'd called him. And soon I found I'd fallen into my same old patterns. I'd stopped fighting a fight I couldn't win, stopped defending myself. I'd let them talk and spread their vile poison until they wore themselves out and decided to retire to their private box.

Neither of them had offered me my usual seat, either. They'd simply turned their backs and walked away. As though I'd disappointed them beyond redemption.

And then there was Tyler, who'd managed to not only spot me from his chair on stage but sent me one of his signature possessive smiles. The kind I would have once melted to receive from him.

Not anymore.

As for me, I'd managed to keep from combusting while I sat through the performance, Gray's large, callused hand in mine, resting on my thigh. Ridiculously close to my aching core and squeezing slightly, the pressure felt through my entire body. He knew exactly what he was doing, and although he kept his focus on the musicians, I knew better. How I wanted him to touch me. A bad idea, since this was a charade after all, but how much worse if we ended the evening without a taste of each other.

One hot glance from him, one stolen touch, and I would go *kaboom*—against all rational thought. We managed to make it through the concert without doing anything stupid —although it didn't stop me from wanting to, even in public —and now we found ourselves at a nearby restaurant. It was one I'd been to several times before after events, with decent food and expensive drinks. Gray, bless him, looked adorable trying to fold his massive body down gingerly into the fragile-looking small chair.

I admired him because I knew he was doing this for me. *Because* of me, because he hadn't liked the way my family had treated me.

No one had ever stepped up like that for me before.

We'd spent a long moment backstage while I said hello to several people I'd worked with during my stint with the orchestra. To show them I was okay? To reminisce just a bit? Probably a combination of both. And I tried my damnedest not to look over my shoulder for Tyler the entire time because I knew he was there. Watching me. Watching us.

At last, Gray pulled me away, practically shaking with hunger, and we'd left for some much-needed food. The man ate all the time. Judging from his muscles and gym routine, he needed constant protein, and I'd had to adjust my meal plans for the family accordingly.

"Do you think we put on a good show tonight?" he asked with a rueful grin. "Tell me the truth. How do you feel about it?"

I raised my wine glass and tapped it gently against his in a toast only we understood. "I'd say we accomplished our goal. My parents were not happy with us." Especially with me, because I was *shacked up* with someone like Gray.

If only they knew the half of it.

He nodded once, looking pleased. "I got the sense they didn't like me," he said with obvious sarcasm.

It took effort to keep from snorting into my drink. "They don't like themselves. Trust me. You could be a Rockefeller and they'd have something demeaning to say about you. Besides, *I'm* the big disappointment for them."

"You?" He stared at me as though he saw straight through my skin to my soul. "You are the complete opposite of a disappointment. And if they don't see you that way, then they can go fuck themselves."

Crass, yes. A little abrasive in his wording. And right on the money.

How would it feel to see the world like he did?

Gray waved a hand dismissively. "They are the least of my concerns. I'm not terribly interested in getting Mitzi and Barney—"

"Bernard," I corrected automatically.

"—to like me. I'm used to being in the spotlight, and with it come my fair share of haters. If I was bothered by everyone's opinion who didn't like me, I'd be a shell of a man and wouldn't ever leave the house."

"You make a good point." The truth of the matter was I'd grown up being force-fed the exact opposite philosophy. What everyone else thought of me, of our family, mattered. Appearances were everything, and my next move had to be dictated according to the view from outside.

What would the neighbors think?

What would the fans think?

I wondered how long it would take me to really stop caring.

"How about your ex?" Gray asked, shooting a small grin to the server delivering three plates of appetizers. "Do you think he got the message?"

I chose one of the appetizers and transferred it to the small plate in front of me. "I highly doubt you'll change my parents' minds no matter what you say. As for Tyler, well..."

Oh gosh, yeah. I'd forgotten about the real reason we'd come out tonight. We'd come out to deliver a statement to my ex as well as to my mom and dad. I sat back in my chair, smoothing the napkin along my lap. Once I relaxed, I found myself having a wonderful time. Wonderful enough I stopped worrying about everyone else and focused solely on Gray as though this was a real honest to goodness date.

I cleared my throat and smiled. But any answer I'd had for Gray was cut short when I saw Tyler Prescott stalking toward us.

He still wore his black suit and tie from tonight's performance. The tie, however, had been wrenched aside to give him some breathing room and there were wrinkles on his cuffs I knew he'd be devastated to show in public on a normal day.

He looked...disheveled.

Gray noticed my distraction instantly. "What is it?"

"The man in question is walking through the door at this very moment," I told him with a slight tilt of my head to the right. Ignoring the tilting of my stomach at the sight of Tyler.

God, would that feeling *ever* go away? We'd been broken up for long enough I shouldn't get this upset seeing him anymore. Right? There must be something wrong with me.

And that was the last coherent thought in my head. Everything else disintegrated when Gray leaned his large frame across the table and kissed me.

He *kissed* me.

His lips captured mine, teasing lightly at first, then his tongue slipping through to tangle with mine in a heated caress.

Oh, *Lord*.

I wanted to keep kissing him all night. Being with Gray while he touched me was quickly becoming my favorite place to be. The restaurant faded away, the people talking and laughing, the clink of silverware and crystal, and the dangerous, predatory stalking of my ex coming ever closer.

The energy of him, of us together...the display left no doubt to anyone with eyes. We *were* something. *Gray and I were something*, even if it was a pretend something. I had to admit it felt very real to me.

Too real for comfort. Because I never wanted it to end.

Gray finished the kiss in his own time and pulled back slowly, his heated gaze dropping to my nipples. Those little double-crossers were rock-hard and straining against the silk of the dress.

"Mmm. You're a method actress, I see," he murmured.

That earned him a hearty chuckle. And managed to ease my nerves a tiny bit.

Tyler ground to a halt at the table and glowered down at us, his dark eyes nearly black with anger. His hands were curled into tight fists at his sides. "Do you have to do that sort of ridiculous display here?" He meant the kiss, of course. "Essie—"

Gray interrupted him, standing up to shake my ex's hand like this was any other meeting. And, I was pleased to note, towering over Tyler in the process. Looking like he could knock the other man to the ground with a single blow. "I believe she's already told you. She's done with you, friend. Whatever she does or doesn't do is nobody's business but her own. Maybe now you'll get the message? The name is Gray Wright. Nice to meet you."

"And now I suppose she's with *you*?" Tyler laughed in Gray's face and refused to accept the outstretched hand. "She'd never be with a *brute* like you. Not in a thousand years."

I wanted to slap him into tomorrow. Man, he *was* a ponce. How had I ever thought him attractive? There was nothing decent about Tyler Prescott. Even his instrument playing was lacking in passion and depth.

What I wouldn't give to tell him exactly that.

"She has been with me and will be again..." Gray paused to look at his watch. "...in about an hour. After we finish enjoying our wine and appetizers."

Man, did he look smug.

Tyler turned red in the face. "You're nothing but a fuck boy. I don't care who you are or how important you consider yourself. You are completely beneath Esther. If she's with you physically, it's only to knock off a piece. And she's had better."

"She had better just yesterday. You can ask her about her multiple orgasms."

As much as I enjoyed the repartee, I didn't like how the rest of the restaurant crowd shifted attention in our direction.

"You son of a bitch!" Tyler blustered.

The name-calling was taking things far enough. It was up to me to stop this before things went in a bad direction and the media caught wind of it. I stood up, lifting an arm in either direction to keep the boys apart. As though I could possibly do anything if they decided to get physical.

"Okay, boys. Calm down. Tyler, we're done and you know it," I told him. "I came out tonight to listen to the symphony play and to see my friends. Nothing more."

"Your friends? Esther, understand this. You no longer have friends here," Tyler spat. He slid his hands into his pockets.

The barb lodged right behind my heart. "You don't know that."

"Oh, I do. Are you aware of what the other strings say about you? They call you a quitter. A lazy quitter who relied solely on her childhood reputation to get ahead and then threw it all away for a cheap lay."

Another smug, rage-tinted grin toward Gray.

I saw Tyler preparing to launch into a tirade to disparage me. To say whatever he could to cut me down and make himself feel better, just as I could feel myself shrinking away from him, drawing into myself because I didn't want to hear any more.

Gray held up a hand. "I'm going to stop you right there before you say something you'll regret. You'll understand, Mr. Prescott, why I'm unwilling to let you continue. There's a crowd here and I'd really hate to damage your reputation beyond repair when I break your nose in front of all these people."

Tyler let out a hiss at Gray's statement. "You wouldn't dare."

"We're done. We are absolutely done." Gray, still standing, pushed away from the table and shifted around to take my hand. "Darling, if you're ready?"

He threw a wad of cash down on the table, more than ample to cover our bill. Good. I wasn't sure I'd be able to stand for much longer without my legs wobbling.

"Yes, let's go," I said to Gray. I laced our fingers together and when I spoke again, it was with more conviction than I actually felt. "I need you inside me within the hour, as promised."

18

GRAY

Esther's sexy as fuck dress bunched up on her thighs as my hands found their way beneath the silk fabric.

We crowded next to each other in the back of the limo, with the partition between us and the driver firmly closed. Sealed and locked tight. No way was some other dude getting an eyeful of Esther and me going at it on the back seat.

And no way was I waiting until we got home to make good on her last statement. The moment the words left her lips I found my cock twitching, getting thick. Ready to be inside of her.

She shifted to straddle my hips as my tongue moved in her mouth slowly. She tasted divine; her tongue danced with mine, sliding against me the way I wished she'd do with my erection.

Her pert nipples pebbled beneath the fabric and her hot core was settled over the place I needed her. Moist. Ready. Aching for me the same way I felt for her. I slid my hands up, up, up—and discovered the woman had been without underwear all night. I let out a groan. *Fuck me.*

Thank heavens I didn't know that back at the concert hall or I'd have gotten us both arrested for indecent exposure for sure.

I leaned back and took in her hooded eyes and her lips puffy from kissing mine. It was a good look on her. She should always look this way.

"No panties, Esther? You're a naughty girl for not telling me." I bit her lower lip. "Do you know what I do to naughty girls?"

She shook her head. Breathless. Excited. "Tell me, Gray."

"Sometimes I spank them." She gasped when I tightened my hold on her. "Sometimes I tie them up. And sometimes," I bent forward to nip at her neck, "I forbid them from wearing underwear for days."

"Like an underwear time out?" Her eyes were big as saucers and her voice held a hint of mischief.

I didn't really have much history with doing any of those things. My sex life with my wife had been decent but fairly vanilla. I wasn't complaining. However, if Esther was open to that stuff, I was all in and excited to try.

"Exactly." I slid my thumb through her wet heat and across her clit. She was so turned on and ready for me. How lucky was I to be with this goddess?

Better for me to remember that while I worshiped her.

"Which one will you do to me tonight?" She leaned in and rested her forehead against mine.

I could tell she liked all the ideas, my naughty minx. Her willingness made me hotter.

"You'll have to wait and see," I replied as the car pulled to a stop outside the house.

I slid her off my lap and she pouted adorably at the interruption. Truthfully, I already had a lot of naked plans for Esther. I wanted to do all kinds of sexy things with her. We could add one or two of those things I'd just mentioned. No problem.

I took her hand and led her up the walk to my house. I couldn't wait to peel that dress off her hot little body and I was beyond happy Sophie and Lucky had offered to keep my kids for a sleepover tonight. When we'd been together last time, we'd needed to be quiet and I was recovering from a head injury. Now we could make as much noise as we liked and explore each other in every room of the house if we wanted.

I slammed the door behind me and she let out a little gasp. I checked my watch. "Twenty minutes until I slide inside your hot little body, Esther." I'd promised her under an hour but I intended to make her wait the full amount of time. Nothing as sweet as anticipation.

"You don't have to wait the full twenty minutes, Gray." She placed one hand on her hip, the silk of the gown doing nothing to hide the delicious curvy body beneath it. I felt bad for the ex for a moment. He'd had this woman and let her slip away. I'd nearly done it too. Then again, he was a massive douche bag and I hoped I wasn't.

"I do have to, Esther. I forgot to tell you it's another way I punish naughty non-underwear-wearing girls who keep that a secret from me. *I make them wait for it.*"

"Seriously?" The pout returned. I wanted to kiss it away. "I suppose I...could take care of myself..."

Holy crap! I really want to see that, but not right now. That we would save for another day.

I snagged her by the wrist. "It doesn't work like that.

Get naked. Get on my bed, and do not touch yourself. I will be right there."

I could see she'd considered arguing but she didn't. She turned and walked at a snail's pace toward the huge staircase in the foyer, swaying that cute butt a little more than usual. This was a game we were playing and we were both enjoying it. She stopped halfway up the stairs and unfastened the dress so that it pooled in silky folds at her ankles before stepping out of it and continuing her lazy ascent to my room in all her naked glory. I'd lost track of who was torturing whom in this slow, tantalizing game.

It took all my strength of will but I waited a full five minutes before I joined her. She was lying naked on my bed all right, flat on her tummy facing the door so that her glorious breasts hung down. I ached to touch them, but first I made a show of undressing very, very slowly.

"Gray!" She moaned.

"You need something, honey?"

"I need your mouth and hands on me right now!"

I stalked toward her in just my boxers and gave that ass a swat just for fun before kneeling before her and lifting up those breasts and sucking on them one at a time. She wriggled and writhed against my mouth.

I dropped her breasts and claimed her mouth as my hands ran up and down her back. She was soft and smooth beneath my calloused hands. When my hand reached her butt, I gave it another swat that had her moaning in my mouth. I didn't really go for anything too rough; the truth was a guy my size had to be careful because my strength could get away from me, but she was enjoying the game, so why not?

"You've been a naughty girl, Esther," I said breaking our kiss.

She just gave me a wicked smile. "Sorry."

She didn't look the least bit sorry and I liked it. Clearly, she'd had people telling her what she could and couldn't do her whole life. I was happy to tell her what to do in bed but only if that was what she was into. Otherwise she was her own woman.

"How are you going to make it up to me, honey?"

"Well, first I'm going to let you inside me so that I come on your big hard cock, and then later I might give you a blow job."

That would definitely work.

I stood and peeled my boxers off; she was still lying on the bed and she was at the same height as my groin so that when I peeled them away, I jutted proudly in her direction. She leaned in and licked the head of my cock in a slow, lazy circle. "Or we could reverse the order."

Tempting though that was, I needed to be inside her. Now.

I hauled her to the edge of the bed and lifted her up so that she was in my arms, standing on the bed. Her luscious curves were pressed against me. I grabbed her ass and kissed her hard. It wasn't a pretty kiss; it was tongues and teeth and hunger. Then I let her go, dropping her on her hands and knees on the bed. Her ripe ass was in the air. And I swatted it again.

"Do not move," I commanded and she didn't as I rolled a condom on.

I returned to stand behind her, grabbed her hips, and entered her in one hard thrust that had her calling my name as her arms bent. What a view, I thought as I pumped in and out of her and she arched her back to get closer.

I reached around with one hand and made three slow circles on her clit and that was all it took. She came, her whole body shuddering beneath me as I pumped in and out again and again until I followed her into a sweet release.

———

I WOKE up with Esther asleep beside me. The sheet was only covering half her butt. I *had* to kiss my way down her spine.

My hands followed the path of my mouth, a feather-soft touch before I kissed my way back up her silky skin, brushing her hair behind her ear, kissing the exposed skin of her elegant neck. She sighed, and I knew she was awake and happy.

I kissed my way back down the path of goose bumps I'd raised on her spine and flipped her over. Christ, she was beautiful. Soft pale curves, ripe full breasts, hips to hang on to. My hands spread her gently open to feast on her pussy. I parted her with my thumbs and took a deep inhale. She smelled like woman and sex. I'd forgotten how much I missed this kind of intimacy.

Her hands fisted in my hair. I had no idea what we were doing here but I couldn't complain when she started my day screaming my name as she came. The sweet taste of her flooded my lips. I kissed my way up her front, stopping to lavish attention on each breast, because how could I not?

"Best tits in the world," I said before kissing her hard. "I need to be inside you again. Now."

She didn't stop me. In fact, she sat up and took the condom from me and rolled it onto my hard cock as I leaned back on my haunches and let her. I've worked hard on this body. She hasn't had a lot of time to really take in all my glory and I watched her hungry eyes travel over me. Not just the proud cock, but the muscular thighs, the ridges down my abdominals, my arms, and wide chest. I licked my lips. So did she.

"You can lick me like a lollipop later, baby. Right now, I need to feel you come on my cock."

"Oh yeah?"

"Yeah." I lifted each of her legs up over my shoulders, and what a view that was as I entered Esther in one hard thrust that had her gasping. I was as hard and thick as I'd ever been. It was a tight fit, the way her channel held me. I paused a moment staring down at her. This was a sight I wanted to commit to memory. Her lying there totally open to me, trusting me with her body. "You are fucking amazing, Esther."

And then I moved. The sound of skin slapping skin filled the room. I went balls deep again and again. I leaned in to suck her nipples and I felt her tighten around me. If I were a betting man, I would bet she'd previously been a one orgasm a day girl, at best; But since she was about to let go again, I supposed it was safe to say she wasn't that way with me. I slid a hand down to where we were joined and my thumb glided across that tight nub of nerves. She let go, yet again gasping my name. I followed quickly after giving a few fast pumps.

I kissed her hard before rolling off, tying off the condom, and tossing it in a trash can by my bed. I'd meant to take it slow and failed. Again.

Then I hauled her against me. She was in my arms where I was certain she belonged.

"We've learned a few things in the past twenty-four hours, honey." She looked up at me, no doubt wondering what those might be. I continued as if ticking them off on my fingers. "That ex of yours was and still is an idiot. That I fucking love that you call out my name when you come. Oh yeah, and you taste like heaven." She was blushing, which, given what we'd just done, was nuts. That made me smile. She was everything. I just didn't know what we were going to do about it yet.

I drifted off with her cuddled in my arms and was woken by sunlight streaming in. Our limbs were entangled, and if the lump in the sheet was anything to go by, I was aroused. Again. When she went to move, I pulled Esther back against me, brushing a soft kiss to her temple.

"I should go before the kids come back." The clock beside the bed said seven a.m. which meant they'd be awake for sure and home any minute now.

"I was looking forward to you licking me like a lollipop," I said, tilting her chin up with my finger.

"As was I." That surprised me but it also made me happy. I got even harder. Again. "I guess we'll have to take a rain check on that."

I sighed. "Later, then."

"Yeah, I don't want to get caught doing the walk of shame back to the pool house," she said, sliding from the bed and grabbing her silk gown from the chair where I'd laid it last night after fetching it as I followed her up the stairs.

But instead of putting on the dress, she just draped it across her shoulder. My eyes grew wide. "You going down there naked?"

She gave me a shrug. "Why not?"

My phone pinged with a text that Sophie and the kids were on their way. Best decision I'd made, taking my sister up on her offer of keeping the kids for the night. She wouldn't ask questions. Actually, she'd probably be delighted to know I'd spent the night with Esther. She'd give me a damn high five.

"Better hurry then," I said as I scrambled into a sitting position. "They'll be here in two."

"*Two?*" Esther half scampered out the door, then ran back, planted a smacker on my lips, and ran out, leaving us both laughing.

The woman really was a little menace.

I wouldn't have her any other way.

Still...I didn't know what any of last night meant. Not a bit of it. We were hot for each other, sure, and the sex was amazing. But in the morning light, she was still my nanny. Still a professional musician wasting her talent, and things were still a mess.

I knew one thing for certain: I couldn't get enough of Esther Richardson and her hot little body. What that spelled out for either of us I had no idea.

In the few minutes I had to spare, I jumped in the shower. As I lathered shampoo in my hair, I wondered what Esther thought of our night together. She hadn't said much about it outside of her sexual demands. Which I both loved and appreciated.

We were definitely hot for each other, there could be no denying that, but outside of the heat...what did she want? Our fake date had stirred up the feelings we'd attempted to put aside. At least, it had for me. In so many ways.

I wanted the date to be real. I wanted her feelings for me, her reactions to me in public to be real.

It was good sex, for sure. But it felt like more.

I craved *more*.

Never had I wanted a woman the way I wanted her. I couldn't get enough. The last two weeks of avoiding her had been torture for me. I mean, it was a big house, but it had been no easy task. Not the least because I was constantly drawn to her and curious about what she was doing. I wanted any glimpse I could get of her beautiful face, her sweet voice, the sound of her laugh.

The word *torture* came to mind.

There was no way I wanted to go through that again. I wanted Esther. The question was...what did *Esther* want?

19

ESTHER

I was all too aware that my night out with Gray had caused a stir when I got the alerts on my phone.

Yet again, I'd become front page news. And this time I refused to let it knock me down.

Once I was back inside the safety of my pool house I set the phone aside with a sigh and focused on getting dressed. The news would be there to peruse at my leisure, just as soon as I made it through the Sophie assault surely headed my way.

Gray and I would need to talk about this whole situation and get our stories straight. As I slid my legs into a pair of comfortable yoga pants, I realized we'd missed the moment. Again. Jesus, why hadn't I grilled him on these things before I ran off?

That seemed to be the story of our entire relationship, didn't it? If that was even what this was between us. Because we never managed to find the time to just talk.

Regardless, the kitchen was filling up with sexy NHL players and their kids by the time I walked the short distance back to the main house. They had descended like locusts, and apparently we were feeding them breakfast if the voice I heard above the chaos was one to be believed. It wasn't Gray. A quick glance showed me Dominik pulled up to the kitchen table, sending me a pleading look, and I rolled my eyes.

Sophie and Lucky were there too, having dropped the kids off, and I was pretty sure Dom and Alexi had come over purely for the gossip. Even Tori came floating in as I was making breakfast, looking like a goddess in a white dress that was more toga than frock.

I might have rolled my eyes at her too, except I knew I had no reason to be jealous. Gray had worshiped me properly last night. So Tori wasn't the only goddess in the room.

I kept the secret smile to myself.

"Well, hey there. Did you two have a good night?" Tori asked suggestively, waving her takeout cup of coffee at Gray and me at opposite ends of the kitchen. He'd snuck in at some point and was now waiting in line behind the children for the waffles I was making. "I hear there was quite a show at the symphony last night, and I'm not talking about the music."

"Subtle, Tor. Subtle." Dom coughed into his hand and I couldn't help the devious smile pulling at my lips.

"In retrospect, I should have offered you my box," Tori mused. "That would have been fun. You two looking down on the musicians like they were beneath you." She closed her eyes. "Yes, I can see it now."

I was glad she *hadn't* offered us the box. Sitting in Tyler's line of sight had been so much more fulfilling. Also, Gray would probably not have kept his hands off me in a private box. Nice fantasy for another time but not what we'd needed for our fake date.

We'd had a hard enough time with that problem after dinner.

"We had great seats, and the performance was..." I trailed off, trying to think of a nice way to describe it.

"Mediocre," Gray supplied for me. He wasn't wrong. "Nothing like the way Esther is on her violin. There was no soul. No life. They were mechanically replicating musical notes on a sheet of paper and nothing more."

"Oh, you're a music expert now, dude?" Lucky inquired, barely concealing his own lopsided grin.

"I know what I like," Gray replied with a haughty sniff.

Great, as if adding more fuel to the fire was a good idea. I flipped another set of waffles onto a plate and had to jerk them out of the way at the last moment to avoid Ryan's reach. Too hot for him; they needed to cool down a bit first.

Like a few other things I could think of at the moment.

Gray wasn't finished. "The music lacked heart. It's just like on the ice. A guy can be technically good but it's that X factor that takes someone from good to great. I mean, you guys know what I'm talking about."

"Of course we do. We all have the X factor in spades," Dom said with mock seriousness.

Dominik might be joking but Gray did make a point. He was right. Lots of people could play the literal notes to a song. Not everyone could create nuance and emotion with their interpretation. Not everyone *felt* their way through the music as though it was a piece of them.

"I don't want to hear about the symphony. I want to hear how it went with the parents," Sophie said.

Dominik waggled his eyebrows. "And I want to hear about the *after*."

Gray met my gaze when I glanced over at him.

"There was no after," I answered quickly. "The fake date went off without a hitch. Here you go, kiddo."

I handed the full plate of waffles off to Ryan and he carried them over to the table to share with the rest of the children.

"Ah, I see. So now you two are basically an item?" Tori asked with a barely concealed chuckle. "Do I need to put out a statement on behalf of the Raiders organization?"

"It's not real," I reiterated, making sure no kids were within earshot. "I'd go with no comment if you're forced to make a statement. Which, judging by the notifications I'm ignoring at the moment, you will probably have to do. We don't want you lying for us."

"Right." Gray nodded in agreement but there was a flash of something in his eyes. Hurt? Anger? Disappointment? We hadn't gotten around to talking about this yet.

Our audience had arrived too soon.

Everyone looked between us and I felt judged. "I'm making more waffles," I said unnecessarily.

"And yet it's not Wednesday." Gray teased a smile from me, an answering one at last returning to his handsome face.

"I'm making an exception. Because I see Dom drooling over the ones I made for the kids. Let's be honest. Who doesn't love waffles? Am I right?" I began to get more ingredients out of the pantry while Tori and Sophie moved to help with plates and coffee cups. Lucky, bless his heart, had already begun a pot of coffee. It would soon be gone. Maybe Gray needed to invest in one of those urn types that made enough brew in one go to satisfy a small army.

Coffee wouldn't help me. Nothing would help me. I was used to this kind of energy and chaos by now, but really I needed to be by myself, to stop over-thinking what happened between me and Gray last night. And more important, I needed to stop sneaking surreptitious glances at him because I knew every set of eyes was on us and everyone had an opinion.

I was sure the girls wouldn't wait to let me know their opinions. Tori was already staring at me with those waggling eyebrows as though she couldn't wait to grill me on all the details.

Thankfully these guys were huge eaters. As if I didn't know before, I sure learned my lesson that morning. You couldn't just give them one waffle and expect them to be satisfied, like the kids now making a racket in the living room. Oh, no. The amount of food required for these athletes was *enormous*. I was pretty sure this breakfast wasn't on any of their approved menus but it was delicious and comforting and belly-filling. As long as I kept the waffles coming, the four brawny men kept their opinions to themselves.

Sophie fried up bacon and sausage for us as well, and Gray, to my surprise, whipped up scrambled eggs as I repeatedly worked the waffle iron. Everyone was talking and laughing and kids were running in and out. It was like a real home, I decided in a flash. A family, even.

Something I'd never had and always wanted. Here it was right within my grasp and I had to keep reminding myself none of it was real. Oh, it sure felt real. It felt like things had finally fallen into place for me.

But it was a lie. A fantasy.

Next to me, Sophie nudged me with her hip to get me out of my head. "No way this is not real."

My eyes widened. "What did you say?"

Was she reading my mind?

"You and my brother," she clarified. "The chemistry

between you is pinging around the room. Wow!" She fanned herself. "Practically enough to choke a horse."

"It is not." I was keeping my gaze trained on the waffles because if she looked into my eyes, she'd see how badly I *did* want it to be real.

"You're telling me you two haven't...*you know.*"

"I didn't say anything of the sort." I blushed and then shushed her. "Keep the *you know* talk to yourself. Little ears and all that."

Of course, she hip checked me again and grinned. The deviant. "Sure, sure. The y*ou know* talk. Don't think you can escape it for long, Esther. It's coming."

I didn't quite get Sophie, I decided right then. Of course, I did not have a brother, but I was pretty sure I wouldn't want to talk about his sex life with whatever girl he decided to date. It was definitely not the way Gray had reacted to Sophie when she'd gotten together with Lucky. I'd heard the stories of him going positively bat-shit crazy a few times.

Judging from the way he'd acted with me, I had little choice but to believe the stories.

I headed to the pantry in search of...well, *anything* to put space between the two of us.

There would be no reprieve in the cards for me. Sophie followed me, and because the house was huge, the pantry was really a storage room, so she shut the door, using her body as a barrier.

"This is great!" she said immediately. Then seeing the quizzical expression on my face, hurried to say, "He would not be sleeping with you if it wasn't *something*, Esther. I know my brother. If you're in his bed then he's serious. I mean it."

"Sophie." I shook my head. "Let's just calm down. I don't want you getting ahead of yourself."

She didn't calm down. No, the woman hugged me instead, and then pulled back and did a little happy dance. It would have been adorable if she wasn't driving me nuts at the same time.

"This worked out just as I planned." She clucked her tongue. "I knew it was a good idea. Just had to wait for the seeds to sprout."

She...*what*? Her words had me doing a double take. "Hold on. You *want* me to hook up with your brother?"

Had she been the mastermind behind this arrangement from the start? And here I thought I'd been hired for my qualifications.

"Duh. Of course I do! You're smart, beautiful, talented, independently wealthy..." She ticked off a list. "Who wouldn't? He's been dead inside since Rachel passed away. He needed someone special to make him take a risk off the ice. You're it. You're the risk, Esther. And you're worth it."

I didn't like the way this conversation was going, or how it made me feel. I especially didn't like the small spark of pure joy bursting to life at her words.

And seriously, me? A risk?

"How do you know?" I asked, flinging the door open to get back before the current batch of waffles burned. Funny how Sophie let me go right by her.

She followed me, of course, and no one seemed bothered about our little tête-à-tête in the pantry. "My brother might be an idiot but I'm not. I had you thoroughly checked out before I hired you. I've seen you perform, as well."

"You have?" Sophie didn't strike me as the symphony type.

"I was dating a guy who wanted to impress me..." She laughed at the memory. "Anyway, I remembered you and the story of you walking away from the symphony. It really stuck with me. I thought to myself, wow, that woman has balls! So when you applied for the job, I already had a pretty good idea about you. I figured anyone who could tough out the kind of schedule like the one you had with the orchestra could deal with the NHL. This isn't the easiest life, you know."

"What are you two beauties talking about?" Lucky shifted over to join us, looping his big arm around Sophie's shoulders in an easy gesture. One he'd surely done many times before.

"We're talking about what an amazing musician Esther is," she answered with a wink at me. "Derek took me to see her perform."

"Ugh, Derek. That dinkus." Lucky actually growled.

Sophie stood on her tiptoes to give him a kiss that was hot enough to fry the bacon in the pan before her. "No need to be jealous," she murmured against his lips. "The *dinkus* is long gone."

"Dude! Absolutely not. Not before breakfast, not in my house, and not with my sister," Gray snapped at Lucky.

But I could tell it was good-natured. I'd come to realize a whole lot of that grumpiness didn't have much steam behind it.

Lucky was slow to break his kiss with Sophie. "Sorry, man," he finally said with an easy smile. "There's just something about her I can't resist."

"Let's eat," I said and everyone clustered around me, appearing from all directions.

I helped the kids who were still hungry load up their plates again and then everyone found a spot around the enormous kitchen table and chowed down. It hadn't taken me long to realize why Gray had needed seating for four-teen people. When his friends gathered, boy did they gather. Fourteen almost wasn't enough.

Dominik started a round of ridiculous knock-knock jokes that had the kids in stitches and I too laughed my ass off. It was the way of things. It was an easy camaraderie and nothing fake about it. These guys had it in spades. It was so easy to see how they all cared for and appreciated each other.

My parents would have hated it.

The thought gave me a rush of satisfaction and I cleaned my plate with gusto.

Alexi patted his stomach when he was done eating. Leaning back in the chair, it was almost easy to see the boy he'd been rather than the badass male he liked to show to the world. "Going to need to lift some extra weights today," he said.

I could almost feel Tori rolling her eyes from across the table. What was it with those two? Maybe one day Gray would spill the beans, because surely he knew. He made it his business to know everything about his team.

Every so often I caught Gray staring at me, when I was pretending not to look at him. I guess we both failed. I mean, it was hard to ignore the hottest guy in the room, one who'd had his hands and his mouth all over me, making me moan and quiver a few hours earlier. The memory brought another blush to my face. Even if I had wanted to ignore Gray, I wasn't sure I was physically able to.

It was even harder when he turned into the tickle monster and chased the kids from the kitchen to the media room to put on a movie for them. Not just his three but the rest of the brood too. He was a natural. Was there anything sexier than a man who was good with kids?

I didn't think so.

"Oh, honey. You've got it bad," Tori said from beside me.

I scoffed. "You're crazy." Still, I couldn't stop watching Gray. "You know what's even crazier? Two rich gals like us loading a dishwasher," I teased. "If the one-percenters could see us now."

"Yeah, but I don't hate it," Tori said with a shake of her head. Her smile was wide. "I actually love hanging out with the guys. Well...except Alexi. That man gets under my skin and he knows it."

"You keep letting him."

"I know! He's hard to ignore. I don't have much to go by, mind you, but it seems like this might be what normal life is like."

"Normal family life. Yes, I had the same thought."

"And you know what? I don't hate it."

"Yeah, you said that. Me either," I confessed. "It's part of why I started nannying."

I didn't get a chance to elaborate because Gray was back in the kitchen and Sophie wanted the gossip.

"So," she slid down the countertop as she spoke, stopping only when she bumped into me, "is what we're reading this time true? You went on a hot date and made the ex very, very jealous?"

She waggled her eyebrows at her brother, who seemed content to ignore her not so subtle meaning.

Dom chimed in with, "And Esther's parents snubbed you, Gray, while autograph hunters were simultaneously hounding you." He took a sip of coffee to hide his mischievous laugh. "That's what I read."

Gray nodded, his arms crossed over his chest. "Sounds about right. Esther's family were not fans of Puck Daddy here, or happy about me being anywhere near their precious girl. They made no qualms about telling her what a brute I am. Wait. Did they use the word brute, or was it Tyler? They blur together."

"To be fair, I wouldn't let you near my daughter either," Lucky chimed in.

"Dude, you've got no legs, you're sleeping with my sister."

Lucky laughed instead of allowing the insult to land. "Yeah, you really should have shut that down before it started."

"You think I didn't try?" Gray held his hands up helplessly. "I blame Dom, he dragged me to the happiest place on earth and I came home to a very unhappy situation."

I'd heard the story already and didn't have any problem following along. In fact, right then I felt as much a part of the family as Sophie.

It was so strange how different it was from anything I knew. I would miss this, I mused. Then immediately shut the thought down before it sent me spiraling into depression.

"*Anyway.*" Sophie was clearly sick of this line of conversation. "I think we all need to hear Esther on the violin. Gray can tell me about the date while she warms up. But a concert is definitely in order."

My heart jumped into my throat and I gave my head a firm shake. "Not necessary. That's not why I'm here."

Sophie pouted at me as if she was used to getting her way in all things. "But I really think everyone would love it."

"Love it they might. It still isn't part of my job description," I replied with a chuckle.

Tori and I finished loading the dishwasher and I popped

the cleaner pod into the machine, then pressed the buttons for the usual settings. There was still a mountain of dishes in the sink. We'd have to deal with them later.

The truth was it felt weird to play for such an intimate crowd. There. I admitted it.

Usually, I had the lights and the stage separating me from other people so that it was just me and the music. Yes, Gray had seen me play, but I hadn't known he was watching. It made a big difference.

The man in question came to stand beside me and leaned close to murmur, "You don't have to play, of course, but everyone would love it."

I chewed my lip. Just like his sister, he was used to getting his way. And I found I had a terribly hard time saying no to him. I'd wound up in his bed, after all. "Would it be weird if I asked everyone to sit with their backs to me?" I finally said.

He grabbed my hand and gave it a squeeze, his entire face lighting up. "Absolutely. Totally the weirdest thing ever. They'll do it."

Oh yeah. The man had found the tiny chink in my armor and took immediate advantage of it.

Which was how I found myself in Gray's massive living room facing the backs of a row of NHL players, their kids, and Tori. My heart was still doing its best to choke me, and my stomach had become a mess of knots, but I held my violin firmly with bow in hand.

"Okay, guys, here we go," I whispered.

I sliced the bow across the strings and began one of my favorite Haydn pieces. Once I let the music flow through me, I forgot all about them. There were no eyes on me to judge me. I was free to be me.

My body began to move to the music in impromptu

dance. Once I finished Haydn, I moved on to the same piece I'd played the day Gray caught me, because I knew it by heart and it was one of my personal favorites.

It wasn't too long, either, because who honestly knew how long the kids would want to listen?

I'd have to take advantage of their short attention spans.

Candace had already balked at the idea of sitting through a concert, giving her father what I thought of as her trademark "whatever," but she still planted herself in a seat beside him to listen.

I kept my eyes closed and played by rote. Except this time, it wasn't a concert for the masses. It was for people I cared about. These people all meant something to me. The music meant something to me.

When I played this more modern style of music, it felt like the violin and I were truly one. It was an extension of me. A seamless extension allowing the world a glimpse into my soul.

Once I started, I let the notes flow through me, moving around the room in a natural dance.

By the time I finished the piece, I was panting.

And every set of eyes in the house was now trained on me. Sometime during the song, they'd all turned around.

Oh, snap.

My breathing was heavy as I took in the crowd and waited a beat. What would they say? Why weren't they speaking? The sheer silence bothered me more than anything else.

Then in a breath, everyone was on their feet whooping and hollering as if I'd scored a goal for the Raiders and not just played them a song on my violin.

"Amazing!" This from Dom, clapping his hands louder than anyone else.

"Breathtaking," Alexi said in agreement.

"You're so cool!" Dom's son, Erik, added as he jumped up and down.

Little Ryan raced up to me and wrapped his arms around my legs in a fierce hug. "That was so great, Esther."

"Thank you, honey."

I looked at his daddy...and it seemed to me like he wanted to do the same. My stomach stopped flipping and a swell of heat settled beneath my collarbone.

"I told you she was epic," Sophie said, proudly speaking as if she was the one who'd discovered me. "And totally wasted in that stuffy old orchestra."

"And being a nanny," Alexi added with an arched brow. "No offense, because you seem good at that too, but come on."

He was right, of course. I set my violin back in its case a little clumsily thanks to Ryan's hold on me.

No matter how I tried to pretend otherwise, Alexi was right. I was running away from my talent in search of a family, and being a nanny was the only way I could instantly get one.

20

GRAY

Later that night, I finally managed to get Esther alone.

It had only taken all day. The worst part? Dom and Alexi had wanted to stay longer, until I'd practically taken a foot to their asses to get them out the door.

Family time, I claimed. My kids needed me.

That, at least, they understood.

And it wasn't a lie.

Candace wanted to stay up late for a family movie night, and because I'd spent so much time away from the kids lately, I was inclined to let her. Georgie won the rock, paper, scissors game and got to choose the movie. It was a cartoon monstrosity we'd seen a thousand times before but somehow, with Esther beside me on the couch and Ryan snuggled in a blanket beside her, I couldn't think of a more perfect scene.

Everything inside of me went steady. Calm. At peace.

I even enjoyed the movie, which was something I'd never thought I'd say. Since when did I actually sit down and *watch* cartoons with them? Georgie laughed loudly at all the jokes and I heard her mother's laugh again.

And although Esther didn't understand the melancholy smile I sent her way, she smiled back anyway.

We got the kids to bed around eleven, much later than their normal bedtimes. It was the weekend and if it meant we got a little more time as a family together, then I'd take it. I'd take them being groggy and grumpy in the morning.

I softly closed Georgie's door around the same time Esther finished tucking Ryan in. The two of us knew better than to disturb Candace once she entered her inner sanctum. She'd bitten my head off before and although neither of them said anything about it, I suspected she had done the same thing with Esther.

My sexy nanny gestured over her shoulder for me to follow her down the stairs. I trailed obediently. Did the woman not know? I'd follow her anywhere. All she had to do was ask.

The nights were getting shorter and the weather cooler now that we'd entered November. Christmas was right around the corner. Should I get Esther a gift? I wanted to get her something no one else would think to get her, from the heart, to let her know how serious I was about her. Jewelry wouldn't impress her, I knew. Neither would anything material.

What if I got the kids together to make a special art project for her?

No way she'd be able to resist me then. She would fall into my arms and never want to leave. Which was perfect because the more time we spent together, the more I wanted her there permanently. Call me brash. Call me irrational. She was my risk, and I knew if I didn't make a move now, I'd lose her forever.

Esther made her way outside into the chilly night and I found the temperature didn't bother me one bit when she turned and wrapped her arms around my neck to draw me close.

"Hi, handsome." She arched closer.

"Hello there, you. What are you doing?" I asked.

"I think you know."

I bent to kiss her, to capture her and taste the sweetness I'd been thinking about all day. Esther undid me. My control left the building entirely. The kisses shifted from sweet to heat, her tongue sweeping to touch mine. I gripped her by the back of the shirt to keep her against me, keep those breasts pressed to my chest. I needed her so much I might have taken her right there.

But before we got to the good stuff, I had to ask.

"Why are you here, honey?" We both knew I wasn't talking about our present location. I meant the entire situation with her nannying and wasting her obvious talent.

"There are...many facets to that question, Gray."

"Then why don't you talk to me about them? It might help to get them out in the open," I urged.

I wanted to know everything, I decided. She was still keeping secrets from me and I'd be lying if I said it didn't bother me.

Maybe if I knew what was going on with her, surprises like the media firestorm around her fake engagement to Tyler wouldn't explode on me like a bomb.

She didn't want to meet my gaze, and if I didn't know any better, I'd say she seemed embarrassed.

No, not my girl. Esther didn't get embarrassed. No one had a stronger spine of steel.

I tilted up her chin until she had no choice but to meet

my gaze. "You can tell me anything. You know that. Talk to me."

It took her some time to answer and she nibbled her lip while debating what to say and how to say it. Her muscles were tense, so I rubbed a trail from her shoulders down the graceful curve of her spine. "Okay. This is crazy, but...all I ever wanted was to be part of a family."

I thought about our meeting with Mitzi and Bernard, nodding in understanding. "I can see how you'd feel that way."

She swallowed a chuckle. "Growing up as a prodigy wasn't an easy path no matter what people say. You know? They think you should be happy for the fame and the prestige. They don't tell you how isolating the experience is. I missed out on so many things."

"While experiencing a great deal of others most people never get to," I supplied.

"I was constantly on the road. Constantly pushed to the next big thing. From the age of eight I had a manager booking gigs for me. Private tutors because normal schooling was impossible with my schedule. No children my own age to play with. No opportunities to just be a child myself. And sometimes when I'd try to call home just to hear a familiar voice, they wouldn't even take my calls. They said it only made the homesickness worse and affected my performance. I wasn't their child. I was a marketable product."

She swallowed hard, so hard I both heard it and felt it, and it sent a wave of emotion through me. No one deserved to go through that alone, least of all a child. To know Esther had been pushed, prodded, isolated...it made me furious.

"You all want to know why I chose to be a nanny?" she said. "Nannying was the easiest way for me to go straight into a family situation without any undue awkwardness. You know? Kind of like a try before you buy deal. It helped break me out of my shell. It gave me the family connection I craved without making things weird."

She paused like she was unsure how to proceed. I hugged her tighter. "Go on."

"I don't want you to look at me differently." Her fingers lightly massaged the back of my neck. "Like I'm some kind of weirdo for my past."

"I don't judge you."

There wouldn't be anything she said to change how I felt about her. If she told me tonight about killing someone in self-defense, I'd commend her for her strength. What did she think was so bad about this conversation?

"The orchestra was my family for the longest time, before I decided to take my life in a different direction. I felt a connection with them that I hadn't felt anywhere else. And then...I just walked away. I made a scene and walked away from them because it was too painful to stay. And if I'm honest, the music had lost its allure."

She broke out of my arms on a shiver.

"Are you cold? Do you want to go inside?" I asked.

Although Esther shook her head, her breath gusted in a white mist. "No, I like the cool air. It helps me think. Keeps me straight." She paused for another long moment before turning back to me. "Leaving the symphony was a tough decision for me, even though I wasn't getting what I needed there. Music was all I'd ever known."

"Did it have anything to do with Tyler?" I interrupted. My hands curled into fists unbidden.

"A little." Esther frowned. "I think I spent a lot of my time convincing myself that my happiness was all on his shoulders. Blaming him for how displeased I was with the orchestra and in our relationship. Make no mistake, he played a big part in my unhappiness. He is a cheating, lying, rotten scoundrel and it took me way too long to see it."

Yes, better. I didn't want to hear her saying anything nice about the man I'd decided to hate. "Sounds like you're still beating yourself up for it."

"A little," she repeated with a dry laugh.

I wanted to break the man's nose. How satisfying would it be to hear the crack of bone and see the blood rush down his weak chin?

There would be an opportunity later, I promised myself. The ponce was bound to mess up eventually. And when he did...I'd be there. Ready and willing to show him I could be the *brute* he'd named me.

Esther wrapped her arms around herself to keep the warmth in. I did what any man should do for his lady and stepped up behind her, hugging her tight until her back pressed to my chest.

"I wasn't the same girl who started playing there, Gray. I'd gone into it thinking about myself in a certain way because I'd been conditioned to think that way."

Maybe I would punch her parents while I was at it. Although I doubted Esther would forgive me for doing so. Then I'd surely be the brute Tyler accused me of being.

"Finally, I'd had enough. I couldn't take living with myself anymore because every day felt like I was living a lie. But once I left...what would I do? What direction could I take? I didn't want to be alone, and being with kids, nannying them, lets me enjoy childhood in ways I'd never been able to. Things like bike rides, cookouts, slumber parties—"

"Hockey games?" I teased.

"Ha. Those too," she said. Her fingers curled into my

shirt when she turned around, craning her face up to mine. "My family didn't do any of those things and I'd wanted them. I'd wanted them so badly. Not only was there no time because of my career, but Richardsons didn't have cookouts. They hosted catered social events I was only allowed to attend to perform. I wasn't part of the family. I was the entertainment."

How did I make her understand? She was already part of *this* family. I wanted to tell her so, and wanted to tell her she was free and welcome to stay. And stay forever.

Crazy, wasn't it?

She'd only been here with us for a little while, a couple of months. It would uproot everyone's lives entirely if she became a permanent fixture. Her parents' lives in a bad way, perhaps, but our lives in a good way. Definitely in a good way.

But it had to be her choice, even though I wanted her to choose us. To choose me.

The only thing I could do was use my body to show her how much I cared for her. Was it enough? I hoped so. I kissed her until I lost myself, and would have thrown her over my shoulder to show her a lot more had she not pushed a hand against my chest to get me to stop.

"I'm sorry to be dropping all this on you," she murmured. "I know it's a lot to deal with."

"It's not," I insisted.

"Guess I just couldn't keep my thoughts to myself anymore. Eventually they start pouring out of my mouth. And I suppose I wanted to...to thank you."

"Thank me? For what?"

Her voice dropped an octave. "For letting me into your home and giving me everything I need or want without me having to ask for it. Because asking is hard since I still have such fear of rejection."

She should never feel that around me, as if she had to be embarrassed to ask.

"You know you can talk to me about anything."

"It's not whether I can. It's whether I *should*," she said.

Apparently, Esther didn't understand—I wanted to be a safe place for her. A safe place where she'd feel comfortable opening her heart. I might get mad—on her account—and I might want to rage at the world for her hurt feelings, but she was free to express whatever she wanted to me. Free to be vulnerable.

I'd be there to protect her. To shelter her.

"Do you miss the music?" I asked because I needed to know. I figured that was the one constant joy of her life, and I needed to find a way to help her keep that if nothing else.

I felt her nod against me. "I do. Playing for myself is amazing, and playing for you and the kids and the guys is better. I really enjoyed myself this afternoon. But..."

"Exactly, *but*."

It was something we both understood. A certain high came with playing for a crowd and the general public. And I knew if I weren't playing hockey, I'd miss it. The rush and the explosion of energy. The connection, impersonal yet deeply personal somehow.

"Is it something you'd like to do again? Perform on stage?"

"That's the thing, Gray." She shrugged. "I guess I'm trying to work through what I really want. Because I thought I knew, but the truth is I *don't* know."

I bent down to kiss her again, listening to her sigh turn into a moan at the contact. The sound was enough to have me nearly lose the rest of my control. But I was strong enough for both of us. If she needed more time, then that's what I'd give her.

I lay awake that night thinking about her and the music, the two of us in our separate beds. Was she still awake? Was she dreaming about me? Esther wanted a family, but she couldn't just walk away from a talent like hers. It didn't come around too often and it would be such a waste to let it wither and die. She might not want to play with a symphony anymore but that didn't mean she had to keep her talent limited to impromptu concerts for me and the boys.

She hadn't had the same kind of childhood Sophie and I had. Not by a long shot. The things we took for granted were things Esther never experienced before.

She probably wouldn't want me sticking my nose into her business, I thought with a chuckle, but that's who I was. I was the guy who fixed things. I was the guy who got things done.

The leader.

I hadn't been given the position by accident. I'd won it through sheer force of will and a logic no one else came close to matching.

When I boiled it all down, I needed to help Esther find a way to have both a family and a career as a musician. Or I had a bad feeling I would lose her.

And hell, I didn't have her to begin with.

My life felt...*complete* with Esther there. Complete in a way it hadn't felt since Rachel was alive. The kids were better for it, I knew. They were happier and laughing more. How long had it been since we'd laughed so freely?

Still, it was selfish. Esther needed to be set free instead of having us like yet another anchor around her neck. It wasn't fair to keep her here, to hold her back, when her talent was meant to be shared. She needed and deserved to be fulfilled.

She needed to play her violin.

I rolled over and punched the pillow beneath my head, although it did nothing to make me more comfortable.

Rachel would have liked Esther, I realized with a start. She'd said she wanted me to be happy and move on, and in that painful moment I'd called her crazy. I'd said I would never meet another woman like her.

And I was right. I knew that, in my hopefully long life, I'd never meet another Rachel.

But Esther wasn't another Rachel. Esther was her own person. Did she not deserve the opportunity to grow, to evolve, without having me and the kids there to hold her back?

No matter how badly I wanted her and no matter how my kids loved her, I knew Esther deserved the chance to move on and be happy, too. It was something to think about. A puzzle.

Would I be able to give her what she needed? Was I strong enough to let her go? To let her choose for herself? And if I actually managed to pull off a miracle, well...would she want to stay?

21

ESTHER

There was something up with Gray.

I couldn't put my finger on what, exactly. I'd sensed it for days but knew it for sure when I set his plate across from me at the dining table for breakfast and he'd grabbed it and ran off to who knew where without bothering to make an excuse. Or even look me in the eyes, which he'd been having a harder and harder time of lately.

Well, *excuse me*. I'd stared after him and had to work hard to keep my jaw from flapping open. It was hard to see how my little bit of honesty the other night was not to blame for his sudden shift in mood.

Shift in mood? Indeed, he was like a completely different person!

He was being secretive and squirrelly on his good days, brusque and dismissive on the worst ones. He didn't want to address me directly and more often than not informed the room at large that he would be staying late for practice.

Yeah, like I didn't sense what was happening. Or like I didn't see what was happening.

It was one of the perks of having the boys live so close to

each other. I saw Alexi's car first, parked in his driveway right on time. Then Dom, when I took Georgie and Ryan for our afternoon walk. Dom zipped home like a bat out of hell and shot me a jaunty wave before bolting into the house.

My eyes narrowed. Sure, right on time. They were always right on time. Except Gray was not with them. He was late.

So what was Gray up to? Did he not think I could see the other guys at home, because we all lived in a two-block radius? That he was *not* staying late at practice like he'd made a point of saying?

Like I said. Squirrelly.

Maybe he didn't care, a nasty voice insisted in my head. He wanted me to see he was late and wonder what he was doing. To torture me.

And of course, my terrible brain kept on by telling me all the reasons why it was my fault he'd decided to distance himself.

I'd opened myself up to him in a really vulnerable way. As my mother often said, men didn't like that kind of *emotional vomit*. It scared them and sent them running for the hills. I'd taken a chance on Gray and look where it got me. It got me a distant man who made it clear he had other priorities—probably a slew of other women, my mind-demon insinuated—and that he only wanted me for one reason.

Sex.

At least, he *had* wanted me for sex. Now he only wanted me to look after his children.

To be the nanny. To do the job I'd been hired to do. So what was I complaining about?

This morning, after Gray had taken his plate and

dashed off like the hounds of hell were chasing him, I felt a tug on my sleeve, glanced down to see Ryan gazing up at me with wide eyes.

"What's the matter with Daddy?" he asked.

Oh, man. Now Puck Daddy's weird mood was starting to affect the children. That was *not* okay. "I wish I knew," I answered him honestly, and then held my arms open for a hug. I gathered Ryan on my lap, moved to the table, and nuzzled the back of his head. "Why do you ask? What do you think is going on?"

Ryan shook his head. "Maybe he's been seeing Mira again."

My heart plummeted. Exactly what I *didn't* want to hear. "Mira?"

"Yeah. He saw her a lot. They would hang out."

I knew what that was code for. And it broke my heart into little tiny pieces.

No wonder he's been late.

"I...I don't think that's what's happening here," I tried to tell Ryan. But it tasted like a lie.

Who was Mira to Gray? How long ago had she and Gray been seeing each other? And why the hell hadn't anyone told me until now?

"I don't know, but he seems mean. Cranky all the time."

I tightened my hug. My insecurities could wait. "Not mean, honey. Distracted. And it's not about you. No matter what kind of mood he's in, it has nothing to do with you. He's just distracted."

"Do you promise?" Ryan asked.

"I promise."

I hoped *that* wasn't a lie.

"Your daddy loves you," I continued. "Never doubt it.

Your daddy loves you and your sisters more than anything in the world."

Not a lie, I thought firmly. And his mood changes had better not have anything to do with whoever Mira was. But something was up.

My nerves skittered daily. Whenever I looked at Gray, I felt them rise in an unsettling way. What if he *was* hiding something from me? He definitely didn't want to meet my gaze whenever he caught me looking at him.

I didn't know whether it was intuition or anxiety telling me we were approaching the end. Not sure I wanted to know, either. The way he was acting...I found myself bracing for the worst.

Two days later he cornered me in the pool house once the children went to bed, dragging me against him like I was the air he desperately needed. Looking at me...

Looking at me like he loved me.

Like he saw me for who I was and not who he wanted me to be.

Which was impossible, considering his recent mood change. I'd thought for sure he was done with me in every way that mattered.

"I've got an away game in Chicago, playing the Black-hawks, and I want you to come with me," he said.

I was so shocked I pushed away and sent him a look over my shoulder, a look leaving no doubt how I felt. "Are you *serious*?"

"Of course I'm serious." Gray crossed his arms over his chest as if to keep from reaching for me again. "I wouldn't ask otherwise."

I heard music in my head, something low and dramatic in a minor key to match the emotion and angst I felt in the moment.

"You've never asked me to come with you before," I said, full of sudden suspicion.

"Just because I never have doesn't mean I never would. I'd like you to be there."

I pushed hair out of my face, trying to make sense of his request. "Who is going to watch the kids?"

"The kids are coming too. We'll get a suite with a kitchen, really go all out."

Ah. He needed the nanny along to watch the kids because he'd be busy with the team. The nanny—*that's me*, I reminded myself.

"Think of it like a little vacation for the five of us. It will be fun."

The five of us. I mulled over the words. How odd. If we were all going to be staying in a suite, then it meant no privacy. There would be too many eyes in such a small space.

My stomach plummeted with disappointment and a sharp pain flashed across my chest. So I'd finally got my wish and our hot fling was officially over almost as quickly as it had began. I'd be going only in an official and paid capacity.

He'd put me in my place with a few innocuous words.

I turned away and fidgeted with something. Anything. "When do we leave?"

"Tomorrow morning," Gray answered quickly.

Glancing over at the clock, I laughed dryly. "Are you kidding? It's already *tomorrow*. I mean today. It's one in the morning."

"Then we don't have much time to try to get some sleep first. We'll have to get up early to pack and catch the flight with the team. Better get some rest." He said it with a small, strained smile.

Nice of him to spring this on me right now. Well, so be it.

"Goodnight, then," I said firmly with a nod as I walked him to the door.

"Yeah. Night."

I didn't sleep much, tossing and turning in bed until the darkness of night faded into a watery gray dawn. Time to get up and pack. I'd have to prop my eyelids open with toothpicks to make it through the day. The exhaustion was enough to make me want to stay in bed. And I never wanted to stay in bed.

Did the kids know we were going on an impromptu vacation? Or was this going to be as much of a surprise for them as it had been for me?

The drive to the airport was mostly silent, with the kids still too sleepy to do much in terms of talking. The rest of the team met us at the airport and a private flight transported the lot of us to Chicago for the game.

I wasn't sure what to say to Gray, if anything. Much easier, I decided, to focus entirely on Candace and Georgie and Ryan. They needed me.

They were my responsibility. It was my *job*.

I also clung to Sophie like she was a life raft in a turbulent sea. We sat next to each other in the friends and family box of this unfamiliar arena. The Raiders were ahead but you'd never know it from Gray's face. Stern. Unyielding.

"They hate the Blackhawks," Sophie told me as we sat among the other hockey wives.

Correction: *I* wasn't a wife. And I had no plans to become one. Not anymore.

"Why do they hate the Blackhawks?" I asked, more just to make conversation than out of real curiosity.

"Because they're assholes. You see number twenty-seven? Bruce Accord." Sophie shuddered. "It seems like the whole team is made up of assholes but he's the worst. The rivalry between the Raiders and the Blackhawks is legendary. My brother always hates when we have to play them. Hates and loves. Sometimes I think the antagonism makes all our players sharper, more competitive."

I watched Gray tense up when the two teams met with the ref on the ice. Number twenty-seven, the main asshole, sneered in Gray's face, and the two of them skated closer until they were nose to nose.

"Uh-oh. Not good," Sophie muttered under her breath.

My blood went as cold as the ice when Bruce Accord reached out to shove Gray. Not one to back down, Gray went forward full force, knocking the other man with his stick before using his shoulder. The ref began to furiously blow his whistle as he inserted himself between the two powerhouse players.

"Oh, wipe the surprised look off your face. Fights happen all the time. You'd better get used to it if you plan on being around much longer."

I glanced over my shoulder at the voice and the woman it belonged to. Brittney something, if I was remembering correctly, married to Seamus on the Raiders. Queen Bitch, the other wives called her. Or something similar.

"I don't see how my face is any of your business," I replied as calmly as I could. Trying for unbothered and completely failing.

Brittney scoffed. Long dark hair cascaded around her face in perfect waves falling down over her obviously fake breasts. Too much makeup, I thought, but that wasn't any of *my* business. "Come on, Esther. That is your name, isn't it?" Her snort told me how she really felt about the name. "It's time to get real. Do you honestly think you're going to last?"

"Last?" A sharp pain began to radiate from between my shoulder blades.

"Yeah, with Gray. He's out of your league and he knows it. Maybe that's why he's not announcing..." She trailed off, waving her fingers between me and him, the fight between the players now over but the tension on the ice still thick enough to cut. "...whatever it is between you two."

Apart from the media frenzy at the symphony we hadn't announced anything, but we hadn't denied it, either. Until today we'd barely been seen together in public since then. Maybe *that* was why I was here, to reinforce the charade.

I didn't want to get into an argument with her. Unfortunately, with the air charged and the buzzer sounding to start the next period of the game, I felt it ramping up inside of me as well. Gray wanted to act a fool and beat one of the other players with his hockey stick? Why couldn't I do the same thing with this former puck bunny?

"One day when you have kids, you'll understand things have to be handled with a certain level of delicacy you obviously aren't equipped to navigate," I finally said with a condescending sniff.

I turned back around in my seat and focused my attention on the game. Determined to ignore whatever she had to say in response.

"I love how you act like these are *your* kids," I heard Brittney reply. "Enjoy it while you can. And for the record, I already do have kids, they're just at home with their nanny. Where they all belong."

I winced. And I know she saw it, but I didn't care.

Sophie's hands were on the sides of my head then. To keep my attention on the whiz of the players around the rink instead of giving in to how badly I wanted to turn around and hit Brittney. Hard.

"Ignore her. She's a bitch on a *good* day. Not sure why someone as sweet as Seamus wants to be married to an ogre like her." Sophie spoke loud enough for Brittney to hear.

No one seemed to care.

"Speaking of ogres," Sophie said in a much lower voice, "what's up with my brother?"

I snorted to accompany the look I sent her. "He's definitely been an ogre lately."

"Yeah, I don't have a clue what his deal is," Sophie agreed. She kept her gaze on her boyfriend Lucky. "Gray hasn't said anything to me."

"Don't you think he's acting a little—" How did I put this? "Odd. Off kilter."

Sophie mulled it over for a moment. "I don't know. I haven't seen as much of him these days as I used to. A little busy adjusting to my new life. Oh, come *on!*" She yelled out the last at a bad call from the referee.

The outbursts at the games didn't faze me anymore. "I can't put my finger on it," I told her. "He's acting distant. He doesn't even want to eat breakfast with me anymore."

"I wouldn't read too much into it. He's a Pisces," Sophie answered, as if that explained everything. "They are *super* moody."

"Really?" I didn't realize grown men in Gray's position had the liberty of being *moody*.

"He goes through these phases where sometimes he is extremely passionate and exuberant, then flips a switch right into withdrawn and subdued. You'll get used to it."

She said it like it was some kind of weather pattern I'd learn to live with.

"Ah, so he's going through a cold period." Or maybe he was truly done with me.

Sophie shrugged. "I don't know. He's my brother but I can't speak for him."

Although I couldn't help but think there was more to the story and she knew what it was.

"Could it..." I swallowed, thinking of the name and feeling sick all over again. "Could it have anything to do with the woman Mira he used to see?"

And there went Sophie, shrugging again. "I mean, maybe. He doesn't talk to me about that stuff. They still might see each other occasionally. They went on several dates a few months ago."

Damn, Sophie! You're not helping.

She didn't know any better. She still thought that Gray and I weren't together because we hadn't come clean with the group. And she said it like she didn't think it was anything serious, anything for me to worry about. But my imagination took the name and ran with it. He *was* still seeing someone else. No wonder he was acting weird with me.

I'd been used for sex again. Just like with Tyler.

Just like with Tyler.

The crowd erupted in a chorus of mixed cheers and boos when the Raiders scored again. They were kicking serious ass today. Lucky made the last shot that sent them over the edge as the final buzzer sounded.

I wanted to puke. Might have puked if the kids weren't there watching me. I had to hold it together for them because they didn't deserve to see me having an emotional breakdown.

I'd never had this big of an issue with anxiety before.

Before Gray.

Because he mattered. He mattered so damn much.

BACK IN THE hotel suite the next morning, Gray might as well have had a black cloud hanging above his head. Even though his team had won the game, his black mood extended out to all of us to the point where Candace suggested we go out for a sightseeing tour and I was happy to oblige her. Anything to get away.

"Are you sure you don't want to come for a walk with us?" I tried one last time to get him to lighten up.

"Yeah, Daddy!" Georgie jumped up and down, ready to release some of her excessive energy. "Come on a walk with us."

"It's promising to be a nice day," I said.

He shrugged. Said nothing outside of a grunt.

Okay, now he didn't even want to talk to me. Great. I decided to ignore him and spent all my energy on the kids.

We finally got home two days later and I was relieved. At least here I could retreat to the pool house and put some distance between Grumpy Gray and me.

"I'll start making dinner in a couple of hours," I told him on our way through the front door. It was my last attempt at trying to carry on as if everything was normal. Another dismissal, another brush-off, and I was going to give up.

Guess it was time for me to start looking for another position. There was no way I'd be able to keep nannying for him if he was going to pursue a relationship with Mira. He certainly wasn't pursuing one with me.

Gray carried in the bulk of the suitcases without complaint. "No rush."

"Chicken parmigiana okay with you?"

He grunted his assent and set the luggage down in a pile at the base of the stairs. Ryan was going nuts now that we were home, running circles through the downstairs, his sneakers skidding on the marble.

"Look how fast I can go, Esther!" he called out on one of his passes. "Do you see me?"

I swallowed hard. "Yes, I see you, sweetie." Then issued a warning to be careful, which he ignored. "I was actually thinking I'd take a few hours to myself in the pool house. Unwind a little. Give you one on one time with the kids."

Gray nodded once, saying nothing. He didn't stop me. Instead, he took his phone out of his pocket and turned away from me. He was always on the phone these days. Texting with Mira more than likely.

Well, I thought, my receding footsteps echoing. *Okay then. Message received.*

The pool house suddenly seemed too small for me. There were music papers scattered everywhere on the small coffee table, my violin case propped against the tiny sofa. The bed I'd managed to make before we left for the away game.

I'd thought Gray and I were making progress on a life together. I might have originally told him no, tried to stop him at every turn, but fate found a way to break down my defenses and push us together time and again.

For what? For my heart to be broken again? I was determined to learn my lesson this time around.

Funny, because I'd known from the jump that I would be hurt if I lowered my defenses and allowed Gray in. I'd fought it, I really had. And then when it happened, it had been so sweet, so unlike what I'd expected, I'd allowed myself to dream again. Dream of a future, a family. Now to have those dreams dashed yet again?

My hand went to my heart at the sudden sharp ache there.

Should I confront him about it? I wondered. I'd tried to confront Tyler, too, to no avail, and I'd blown up my career and my ties to the orchestra as a result.

No, it was better to simply exit the situation with dignity. While I still had some dignity left.

Time to accept the facts and move on. Time to start seriously looking for new employment.

22

ESTHER

The call could not have come at a worse time for me. There were already so many things to think about, so many things to do, I didn't have a spare moment to go and check out this school where the director wanted to install a music program.

Except...it was exactly what I'd thought about. Like those secret dreams in my head had somehow manifested into this opportunity. And the reason why I had wanted a good paying job.

I wanted to use the money to set up programs like the one the school director was proposing, programs for under-privileged youth to receive music lessons for free. Why shouldn't those kids get the same opportunities as everyone else? Their parents might not have the funds but children grew better, were happier, when they had access to music.

It was the only thing that had gotten me through my own less than stellar childhood.

I'd been stewing over the idea for a long time, and had told Tori and Sophie about it during one of our late-night gab sessions at the Swirled Squirrel.

The school director, Mr. Thomas, was one of Tori's contacts.

Trust the woman to find the right strings to pull. She really was an angel.

Now the opportunity fell in my lap. And what was I doing? Worrying about how to make time in my busy schedule. Or not so busy schedule, really, because who was I fooling? All I was really doing was killing myself by stressing over situations I had no control over and worrying about Gray's change in behavior.

Maybe it was time to take a little bit of control back for myself. *Stop being weak! He's done. Get over it.*

I slipped into the car and zipped downtown, trying to figure out the address Mr. Thomas had given me. I wasn't the best with directions but I had a feeling where to go.

"You're driving too fast!"

I nearly jerked the car off the side of the road at the sound of the voice coming from the back seat. Tightening my hands on the wheel and trying to get my heart back in order, I spared a glance in the rearview mirror and saw Candace's sleepy eyes staring at me.

"Candace! Do you want to explain what you're doing here instead of being in school?" I asked, insanely happy when my voice didn't shake. "And no excuses," I warned her. What was she doing? And how had I not noticed her in the first place?

She at least had the decency to look guilty. "I didn't feel like going to school. I snuck in here to avoid the school bus and I guess I fell asleep."

"Why didn't you feel like going to school today, Candace?"

"I...I had a test. I didn't study for it."

I sighed, taking the next left turn. "You should have talked to me about this."

"Why would I talk to you?"

"Why wouldn't you?" I tried not to feel insulted.

"Umm, because you're my nanny," Candace said with an eye roll her father would be proud of.

I nodded. "Yes, I'm your nanny. Which simply means I'm here for you. I'm here for you to talk to when you need an ear, or when you need someone in your corner. It also means there will be consequences for you skipping school today."

Candace groaned. "Oh, come on, Esther."

"No, I'm sorry. It was wrong for you to skip because you didn't study. I didn't say the consequences would be horrific, only that there will be some."

I'd have to talk to Gray later. But the thought of him had my stomach souring as I took another left toward the school. I flipped the blinker. Gray would have to wait.

"Where are we going?" Candace finally asked.

"We're going to talk to a man about a music problem," I told her.

"Do you even know where you are right now?"

I glanced down at my phone and the GPS app running. "I'm figuring it out."

I didn't have time to turn around and drop Candace off at school. Nor at home, since she would be there alone without supervision. Nope. She would simply have to come with me.

She didn't seem to be complaining.

Eventually we pulled into a nearby parking garage packed to the brim with midmorning traffic. Most of the spots were full. The school wasn't in a bad location just outside of downtown but it didn't exactly leave us enough room to pull right up to the front door.

"Stay close to me," I told Candace as I locked the car behind us.

She rolled her eyes again. "I'm not a baby."

"It's more for me. I'm nervous, and actually I'm happy to have you here. As a little moral support."

She seemed to weigh my words before nodding once and walking at my side. I'd take it as progress. And no way was I going to leave her alone.

Then my heart constricted. Progress for what? I'd be resigning soon. Maybe she'd be happy to get a new nanny, one who would let her get away with more.

The street was noisy when we exited the parking garage, heading right toward the middle school. I walked closest to the road, making idle and easy conversation.

"Why are you doing this, again?" she wanted to know, interrupting my fascinating discussion about the weather.

I glanced her way and decided to tell her everything. "I believe with all my heart that music helps people. I also believe everyone should have access to learning about music and playing an instrument regardless of where they live or where they come from," I said.

The traffic made me want to reach out and take her hand, to keep her close. Candace would hate me if I even tried.

"That's actually really nice," she replied.

The comment warmed me. "A lot of kids in areas like this don't have the funds or the access to lessons. I figure if I have the money to help implement some programs, then why would I not help?"

"I think if you have a lot of money, you should give back

to people who don't," she told me, scrutinizing the street. "It seems right."

My heart melted a little further and I was surprised I hadn't turned into a puddle of goo on the sidewalk. "You're right, sweetie."

We made it up to the front gates of the middle school. Surrounded by high fencing on all four sides, the two-story brick building was not in bad shape considering its location. The fence was worrisome but I understood the necessity.

It was a far cry from Gray's children's private school.

"I guess it's easy for me to get lessons because of who my dad is," she said as she turned her attention to the school. "But it isn't always that easy for other people."

Was I mistaken? Or did I see a small smile on her face?

"Exactly," I said lightly. "I want to help kids, kids who aren't so different from you, embrace learning an instrument. It might even keep them out of trouble."

I sent her a wink to let her know I wasn't talking about her. Although we'd have to have a talk about skipping school.

Together we walked through the front gate and into the school.

The meeting went better than I could have expected. Candace sat next to me the entire time, interjecting when she thought it was necessary and bringing a smile to Mr. Thomas's face. We discussed the logistics of my donation and program implementation. It wasn't as far-reaching as I'd hoped—one school, a few different ages—but it was a start.

I had to remember: you started at the bottom and you worked your way higher. One step at a time.

It was the beginning of something new and a great way to spend my money. *My* money, not Mitzi's or Bernard's or anyone else's. Money *I'd* made doing something I truly wanted to do, off the stage.

I clung to the thought.

I'd need something to focus on to get me through these next few months, especially if Gray tried to kick up a fuss about me leaving—and I had a terrible feeling he would.

I drove back to the house with Candace in the front seat, safely buckled in and finally opening up about school and why she didn't study for her test.

I wanted to cry.

We decided to stop for a quick snack on the way home, and by the time we pulled into the driveway, I'd gotten her to laugh at one of my jokes. Candace was actually laughing with me!

Why did I have to leave?

Two days later, I should have been packing or talking to my banker about my donation to the school.

I did neither.

Of course, I'd never just walk out and leave Gray in the lurch, so I decided it would be best to let Sophie know she needed to hire a new nanny. She'd been the one to hire me, after all. The problem with my plan was that I knew how Sophie would react when I told her. She would try and talk me out of it because she had stars in her eyes.

Unfortunately, I knew better than to gloss over the details of reality. There were red flags and those should not be ignored.

Yay for her, though. She and Lucky had found each other *and* love. Their story did not, however, set Gray and me up for our own happy ending.

I was tired, and I was sad.

Would I lose all my new friends if I left? It was a legitimate concern and one I could not ignore. Maybe the girls would still meet me for drinks every now and then at the Swirled Squirrel.

I liked to think so, but then again it was a fantasy I'd do well not to lose myself inside. Sophie might not forgive me for leaving, but I hoped Tori would be able to see things from my perspective.

And what about the kids? *Finally*, I sensed Candace was actually starting to like me, which meant her sister was allowed to like me. Little Ryan... I sighed just thinking about saying goodbye to him. The little punk was adorable. Him I would miss almost as much as his daddy, which said something.

Not the cold, closed-off Gray of the past week, but the one I had gotten to know earlier.

The thought of leaving had my heart clenching until the pain became an ache I could not ignore.

Sitting there staring out at the pool and its sparkling blue water, I realized...somewhere along the way, I'd lost my own sparkle. I hadn't really had a break from work in, well, forever. I had been kept in constant movement from age six.

I shifted away from the window. I'd always chased the gold ring. Even here, the gold ring was a place to belong, and I'd thought I'd found it. Turning, I glanced around the little pool house I'd claimed as my own. A safe haven much like the apartment I'd given up to take this job.

And yet I'd lost another family. One I'd hoped might be forever. It was almost too much for me.

Maybe I would not look for a new job right away.

I don't need the money, after all.

Perhaps I'd go sit on an island beach and drink cocktails all damn day. It couldn't do more damage than Gray had. Except I was not sure what I'd do with all the time to *think*. Bad idea. It sounded dangerous.

Pretty sure my mind would just wander back to Gray and the feel of his lips against mine and his hands on my body and...and everything he ever did with me.

Ryan appeared in my doorway with a smile on his sweet face. No knock. He burst right in like he owned the place. Which in a way I supposed he did.

"Hey kiddo, what's up?"

"Are you busy, Esther?"

I spared a glance to the couch where I'd planned to sit and sulk for a while. "Do I look busy?" I kept my tone light and joking.

"It's hard to tell with adults sometimes," he said, his tone serious.

I couldn't help but smile. "True. I'm never too busy for you, Ryan. What's going on?"

He held his hand out to me. "Can you come with me, please?"

Curious. "What's up?"

He gave his head a small shake. "It's show, not tell. That's what my dad said."

His dad? I had less time for and far less inclination to see his dad, but I'd told Ryan I'd go with him. I was committed. Honestly, how could anyone say no to a face like his?

He led me across the yard, past the pool, and through the sliding doors to the ground floor. Then he took a sharp turn toward the basement stairs, gesturing for me to hurry up. I'd rarely gone down there because it's where the gym was, and it always felt like Gray's domain.

Ryan was fed up with my slowness and ran back to grab me and drag me along.

"What's the rush, buddy?" I asked breathlessly as he tugged me down the stairs.

"You'll see!"

He pulled me around a corner and I did see. Or I thought I saw, because I didn't quite believe what I was looking at.

"Ryan..."

What I'd expected, I was honestly not sure; maybe a Lego castle or a train track. Definitely not a brand-new music studio complete with soundproof walls.

Before me was a production studio in all its glory. There was a production room for edits, with a mixing deck and who knew what else, and on the other side of the glass was a soundproof recording studio complete with microphones and a variety of musical instruments.

Gray and the girls stood inside the studio with matching grins on their faces. My heart stopped completely.

Ryan tugged my arm again and his excited voice yelled, "It's for you. We built it for you! Do you like it? Say you like it, Esther."

"For *me*?" Looking down at him, I couldn't quite make sense of it all. I lost my ability to form words.

What did he mean, it was for me? When had this happened?

Across the room, Gray barked out a laugh. "Calm down, son. I think you're scaring Esther."

"No, I mean..." I trailed off, wanting to laugh and cry and scream all at once. Not sure which reaction would be more appropriate.

"Hey." Gray closed the space between us and stood in front of me. He placed his hands on my shoulders and only then did I realize I was trembling. "I thought you should have the best of both worlds, make your own music and recordings *and* have a family that loves you. If you want us, that is."

Those eyes bore into mine and I floundered as if drowning. I lost what was left of my resolve to leave.

"Gray, I...I don't understand—"

"So I see. I wanted it to be a surprise. We've had to keep you distracted for a little bit."

All his mood swings were to keep me distracted? No, it wasn't possible.

Was it?

"I thought you were done with me," I whispered, because the kids were right there, their faces full of expectation.

Although I didn't mean to let it slip, a tear leaked from my eye and he wiped it away with the pad of his thumb. There was the caring man I'd missed. The gentleness I'd thought I wouldn't see again.

"I'm sorry. I guess I was so distracted by getting this done and keeping it secret, I forgot to be there for you." Gray pulled me in for a big hug.

I clung to him. I couldn't help myself. He smelled so good, and if what he was saying was true then this was good news. This was the *best* news.

This was the news I hadn't dared to dream about.

"Okay, start again. Use all the words," I ordered him.

He turned me in his arms so that I faced the studio, placing one large hand on each shoulder to guide me forward. "This is for you, Esther Richardson. We all want you to stay with us but we also know you need to make your music, your way. The world deserves to hear it, and you need it to be happy. So we built you a studio. Now you can work from home."

I looked around at the space and it was pure perfection. "It's beautiful."

"You can make videos for online streaming or you can

record a whole album, whatever you want. By the way, Tori said she'd invest in a new record as well, if that's something you're interested in pursuing. Or you can just use the space for your own hobby and enjoyment, knowing we all love you and want you to stay here and be happy."

I turned back to him, needing to get one more question off my chest. "As the nanny?"

He shook his head. "As more than the nanny." He brushed a soft kiss across my lips, and behind him the children oohed. But...they didn't sound surprised or repulsed. If anything, they were excited.

"We talked about this as a family," he said, "and we all want *you* to be part of *our* family, if that's what you want too."

"You...y-you do?" I met Candace's eyes first, then Georgie and Ryan. The oldest didn't exactly look thrilled but she nodded. Ryan was practically jumping up and down.

"They do. Now we're waiting to see what you say." Gray tightened his grip on me. "How about it? Do you want to be a permanent fixture of the Wright household, Esther? And *not* as the nanny."

I looked around at the kids again, who were all looking at me expectantly, even Candace. Waiting for my answer. "I have never wanted anything more in my life," I told them.

Then Gray whirled me around to face him, his lips crashing down on mine. Thank goodness he kept the kiss G-rated. Well, maybe M-rated, because I heard the girls groaning in the background.

Then the children rushed forward as a unit to throw their arms around our legs and waists in a group hug.

Gray shook his head. "I can't believe you thought I was done with you."

"You've been distant and secretive, Puck Daddy. You're going to have to get better at using that mouth of yours for more than kissing," I whispered against his lips with a final, decisive peck. "Like, you know, *talking* to me."

"This mouth is good for a whole lot. I'll show you later." Warmth curled in my belly at the words he whispered. Oh, I had no doubt about *that*. "And I promise I will do better. Every day, better and better," he continued. "I was so busy getting all this done—and multi-tasking isn't my strength, except in the bedroom."

I broke his hold on me enough to give me room to face the kids. I said with mock sternness, "You three! I can't believe you kept this secret. You guys are all so sneaky." I was going to have to keep my eye on these monkeys, for sure.

"Dad promised us money if we kept quiet," Candace informed me. "It's probably terrible parenting to bribe your kids, right?"

I loved that kid and her sass. She wasn't wrong, but now wasn't the time to go into a lengthy discussion on bribes. "Depends how much he promised you," I replied.

The number she repeated was crazy, astronomically high. No wonder she'd kept her mouth shut. I couldn't help but grin. Such a Puck Daddy move.

I burst out laughing. I couldn't wait to see all his moves now.

EPILOGUE

GRAY

I stood in the door to the studio, watching Esther rosin her violin bow. It was late now, and the kids were all zonked out in bed. Keeping this secret had clearly exhausted them. I had to admit pulling this off had left me kind of spent myself.

And more than a little terrified. Only now, after she'd explained to me how she'd been feeling, did I realize how close I'd come to screwing things up with Esther permanently. She was planning to leave me because she thought I didn't want her. My heart hurt at the thought of it.

I'd been so focused on getting this project done and getting through my hockey games I simply hadn't spared a thought to what she might be thinking. There were too many other things on the plate to juggle.

I'd hurt her, albeit unintentionally.

I got it, though. I did. We hadn't had a lot of time to build trust between us and she wasn't used to being appreciated the way she deserved to be. And maybe, just maybe, I'd been too focused on getting this done to show her that appreciation in a consistent manner.

I made a vow to myself then: I would always make her feel that way from now on. No exceptions.

Starting immediately.

The sexy vision that was Esther called out to me like a siren song. She was instantly at home in the studio, setting up her violins on stands. Yes, multiple violins. It turned out she had several instruments she hadn't brought with her when she'd first moved in, and we'd immediately arranged to have them collected and delivered.

In the past few hours, we'd hosted an impromptu engagement party with all our friends. It had been fun and amazing, but I was sad her family wasn't here to see how happy she was. How she glowed.

Esther was finally being loved right.

"You're my family now," she'd told me when I whispered that to her, snuggled on the couch surrounded by our friends and their kids. "They don't matter anymore."

Except I still wanted to punch them both in the face, right along with her trashy ex-boyfriend. Oh well. There was plenty of time for violence later. I wasn't planning to actually hurt anyone—unless they tried to hurt my woman.

Right now, Esther was bent over so her perfect ass was pointing directly at me. I wanted to walk over and squeeze it. I wanted to take her here, but I controlled myself. There was time. We had forever.

Still, tough to do.

"You like the space, really?" I asked, already knowing the answer as she'd made it clear a dozen times already.

She glanced over her shoulder at me. "You know I do. I really don't know how to thank you, Gray."

"You don't have to," I said. Truly meaning it with every fiber of my being. I'd wanted to do something special for her. "Though I would love to hear you play."

"Really?" Her face lit up. "Now?"

I was not really a fan of classical music, but that's not all she played, and I was a *huge* fan of her and the way she looked while playing, so happy and so complete.

"Yeah, maybe you want to give me a solo performance. Naked. We can christen the studio. Break it in right." I flashed her a lecherous grin. Things had happened so quickly; we hadn't had a chance to do our due diligence with the space. Between games and our hasty engagement and the kids...

A pretty pink blush climbed the column of her neck. I looked forward to kissing that later. "Okay."

"Okay?" Hmm, easier than I'd expected. I'd only been half-serious about the naked part.

"Sure, as long as you're naked, too."

Without any further hesitation, Esther peeled off the t-shirt she wore and the shorts soon fell to her ankles. She kicked them aside and stood there in a white lacy bra and a matching thong.

I lost my ability to breathe, mouth going completely dry. Yes, she was a vision. When she removed them to bare her whole self to me, I had to force in a breath before I passed out. Already there were black dots dancing in front of my eyes.

"You...you..."

She tilted her head my way, gesturing for me to do the same, and I quickly shed myself of all my clothing and took a seat on a cushy chair by the door. The door which I'd had the foresight to lock.

The room was soundproofed so we could be as loud as we liked. That was a bonus I'd only just thought of. And the thought made me even harder.

Esther bent to choose an instrument from her extensive

collection, her back to me, and I put my hands on my thighs to keep myself in check. *Be a good boy, Gray.*

At least for a little while.

With her back to me she straightened and tuned the violin. She and the instrument were perfectly matched, her perfect body all sleek curves.

She turned to face me and licked her lips. She might be nervous, but it was sexy as hell and my already hard dick twitched.

"I've never done this before," she said softly.

"One of many firsts for us," I replied, the emotional gravel in my voice evident.

Then she started to play. I didn't recognize the tune, which was no surprise. It was slow and sexy and she swayed with it. Her ample breasts swung gently and I watched as the peaks hardened. She looked amazing and it was clear she was aroused too. Her eyes caught mine and she took a couple of steps closer, still out of reach. I fisted my cock because I was only human and her eyes traveled to my hand.

She came to sit on my lap, straddling me with her back to my front, my very hard cock pressed against the softness of her ass. I reached around and tweaked her nipples and her rhythm faltered the tiniest bit but she didn't stop playing. She moved, and I held those delicious breasts in my hands as her ass rocked against my thighs. Hottest thing I'd ever seen or felt.

I reached down between her thighs to her apex and ran a finger there. She was wet and ready for me. I loved the music and how it made her feel but I needed her now. How long did this song go on? I could hear a crescendo building. Her swaying became more intense and she moved that bow across the instrument faster and faster. I mirrored the rhythm with my own hand. And then she reached the apex of the song and as she did, I lifted her hips so that on that final note I lowered her down onto me and she cried out, finding her own sweet release.

She lowered her instrument slowly. Panting on my lap.

"Sexiest woman on the planet," I said as I bit her earlobe, lifting her up and down my cock until I came, seeing stars. Feeling the woman I loved clenching around me. Esther and I fit. It was a cliché but it had to be said: "I think we just made beautiful music together, honey."

That earned me a soft laugh. "I think we have a whole symphony in us, Gray."

I was a hockey player, not a musician, but I was happy to keep practicing making music with her forever.

"Don't be nervous!" I told the kids.

At least, the kids who'd been able to come.

Most of their parents had agreed once I'd told them I was sponsoring the trip to Disney World, but I understood why others had put their foot down. A lot could happen on vacation, especially in the happiest place on earth, no matter how many waivers I had them sign or how many assurances I made.

The sad truth? The kids in my violin class were easy as pie to wrangle.

My own kids were the problem.

"Georgie, please stop climbing the lamppost!" I wanted to tug my hair out.

We were slated for an afternoon concert in the Magic Kingdom in approximately... I glanced down at my watch. Ten minutes. Ten minutes to try and get their nerves under control.

Get mine under control as well.

Then Gray was there behind me, with his fingers lightly pressing against the small of my back in a show of support.

"You worry about the performance," he leaned close to tell me. "I'll get the little monkey down from the lamppost."

"Thank you."

He bent to kiss the side of my cheek and I sighed, closing my eyes.

It was really damn hot out here.

Happiest place on earth, sure. The lines were a bear to deal with and the five other children who'd been able to make the trip were a handful.

But I wouldn't trade any of this. Period.

It was Gray's second time here, and when I'd told him my idea about bringing them all with me for an impromptu family vacation, he'd scowled. His gaze went dark and he'd muttered under his breath about a former disaster and coming home to tragedy.

And by tragedy he meant his sister and Lucky.

I tried to tell him there were no surprises waiting for him this time, that everything would be smooth sailing.

He didn't know about my positive pregnancy test yet.

I was keeping that news for when we finally got back home and had some alone time.

Boy, he was going to be shocked.

I clapped my hands for attention. "All right, guys, listen up," I told my students.

There were two other chaperones from the school floating around someplace. Distracted, more than likely.

"I want you to remember, above everything else, to have fun." I smiled around at the nervous thirteen-year-olds clutching their violins to their chests. "We've been practicing for this concert for six months. Ten songs, thirty minutes, and you are going to be terrific."

I prayed they believed me, because I truly had a gut feeling this was the first public outing of many to come. I had big plans to work with Mr. Thomas and the other school districts to implement similar programs. More kids, more families affected. More children with access they didn't previously have. If I could make this a statewide deal, then I would.

It never hurt to dream big.

The students began to cheer and I spared a glance over to where Gray was currently trying to pull Georgie down from where she'd climbed almost to the top of the antique-looking black lamppost. As if feeling my attention, he briefly glanced my way and winked.

I winked back.

"It's show time!" Ryan yelled out.

I bent down to kiss the top of his head and wave to Candace before walking to the front of my group and drawing in a deep breath.

Show time.

The feeling never got old.

I spared a quick glance toward Gray, blowing him a kiss, then stepped forward to the sound of applause.

Feeling, for the first time in my life, I'd really earned it.

THE END

Continue the Minnesota Raiders novels with Dominik's story in Single Shot.

For author updates, sign up for Eden's newsletter
www.edendunn.com

ALSO BY EDEN DUNN

The Minnesota Raiders

Lucky Shot

Hot Shot

Single Shot

Last Shot

Second Shot

Slip Shot

Snap Shot

Penalty Shot

Stolen Shot

Crack Shot

The Arizona Rattlesnakes

Match Made

First Match

Bad Match

Best Match

Re Match

Un Match

ABOUT THE AUTHOR

Eden Dunn is a joint pen name for two USA Today Bestselling authors who have combined their skills to write hockey romances hot enough to melt the ice. Together they are an indomitable force who love a good happy ending, a dirty sex scene, and strong coffee.

If you love enemies to lovers, forbidden love, single parents, and emotional healing, then you're covered! These hockey heroes are the stuff of fantasy because they are hot, hard, and have hearts of gold, while the heroines are strong, sassy, and smart. With take-no-prisoners characters and gripping stories, Eden's contemporary hockey series will knock your ass on the ice and claim your heart.

Sign up for the newsletter to have insider access on new releases, sales, and giveaways.

Choose your favorite team, the Raiders or the Rattlesnakes, and join the fun!

WANNA KNOW MORE?

Hey sexy reader! Want to find out more about Lucky and Sophie? Check out Lucky Shot. Here's a little snippet for you:

MY NAME IS LUCKY.

And that's exactly what I just got.

Of course, I wasn't *born* Lucky. I was born Luke Price in Cincinnati, Ohio, on a bitterly cold night in January. The moment I got signed on as a rookie to the Minnesota Raiders hockey team, things changed, starting with the name. I hit three between the legs shots in my first game and managed to score a whopping 50 times in my first season.

Thus the nickname.

I put it to good use, too. Coupled with good looks passed down from my mother's Italian side of the family, I had the combination of dark hair and swarthy olive skin to help me get my way both on the ice and between the sheets. Being a good person gets you far, it's true, but being *good-looking* opens more doors. My father taught me how to use charm and charisma to my advantage.

The sweetie I'd just sent on her way certainly seemed to agree with my nickname, if the saucy over-the-shoulder smile she gave me was any indication. It was September, and the weather was decent enough that she didn't need a coat to cover up. All that smooth skin in a tiny little cropped shirt and a pair of low-slung hip-hugging jeans—

"See you soon?" she asked.

I hope not.

I waved her off instead of answering because I didn't trust my voice. At least the toothy grin was genuine. "Sleep well," I purred.

Sorry, sweetheart, but I don't roll with the relationship train, period. I also don't usually invite my one-night stands home with me.

It was the off season, I reasoned logically, watching Whatever-Her-Name-Was walking out to her car. Off season meant I was in relaxation mode and tended to drop my guard lower than it should go. I had a few more weeks before hockey season started. Damn if I wasn't going to milk the free time for all I could.

I'd taken a chance on this one and asked her home with me after we'd knocked back a few beers at the local bar. She'd been suitably impressed with the gated community, as well as the way-too-big house I'd bought last year. Hopefully, my poor judgment wouldn't come back to bite me in the ass.

The door swung silently closed behind her and I stretched my arms overhead, muscles loose and limber, feeling like a million bucks. *Hell yes!* Nothing like a little sweaty sex to get the blood pumping. It was one of my favorite ways to work out and keep the heart rate high, outside of the gym or the rink.

No one had better luck than Lucky Price. Both on and off the ice. I pumped my fist high overhead because hell, why not. There was no one around to see the impromptu victory dance.

A knock at the door took me by surprise and I turned toward it, scowling. *God, a clinger. Shit.* I'd brought home a clinger. And *this*, I reminded myself with a mental slap, was why I didn't bring ladies to the house. It was always better to go to their place or meet in neutral territory like a hotel.

Lesson learned.

Then again...

I lived in a gated community. What were the chances the girl had made a swift turn-around and come back? Did I have to have a talk with the gate guard to make sure once these chicks left they stayed gone?

I waited through a second round of knocking before deciding I was going to open the door, approaching it as though a dangerous animal was on the other side. There might be, for all I knew. A dangerous animal who would demand breakfast in a few hours. I couldn't even cook eggs.

She probably wouldn't see it as a viable excuse.

"Sweetheart, I'm worn out—" I began.

Then I stopped when I pulled open the door. There wasn't a woman standing on the porch. There wasn't *anyone* out there. I looked out onto an empty street and the softly glowing lamp across from me in front of the neighbor's house. No girl, no Grade A Clinger.

"Damn kids."

I didn't see the car seat until I almost had the door completely closed. Didn't hear the sigh of the baby inside the car seat until I settled the pounding of my pulse in my ears.

And as I gazed at it, the plastic seat seemed as if it grew to the size of an elephant. How had I missed it? And how had it gotten here?

More important...who was inside?

My stomach dropped and did a back-flip into the deep end of polar icy waters.

No sign of a woman, and I sure looked. Craning my neck around either side of the doorjamb, I did my best to ignore the car seat and the cooing baby inside despite the way my stomach flipped.

"Hello?"

My voice echoed back to me. There were no vehicles parked along the road, either. Finally, I glanced down at the pink-blanket-wrapped elephant in the room. Or rather on the porch.

The baby stared at me now, too, blinking fiercely, with little hands balled into fists. It wore a faded pink gown, and its abundant black hair shot out at all angles.

No woman, I thought as I surveyed the area again. But there was a note.

"Well, hi there..." I cooed, creeping closer to the baby before plucking the piece of paper off the blanket across its lap. "Excuse me."

The baby said nothing. How old was it? Could it talk, or was it ignoring me the same way I tried to ignore it?

The dim light made it impossible to read the tiny scrawled words of the note. I flipped on the porch light until it became clear. A pain started beneath my sternum and traveled right up to my head when I recognized the writing.

Shit indeed.

Lucky,

I thought this was what I wanted, but it is so hard. You didn't want to keep me, but I wanted a piece of you and did what I had to do to make it happen. I didn't realize how much work came with a baby or how lonely I was until I met someone. He's an amazing, wonderful man, except he doesn't want kids. And it turns out I don't either. It's too much.

I really love the guy. And you know I'm not good at being alone, so Lucky, meet your daughter, Natalie. Sorry about just dropping her off but I knew you wouldn't want to talk to me. We didn't exactly end things on a high note, did we?

All the paperwork is in an envelope tucked beneath the blanket. I've signed my rights away. One look and you'll know she's yours.

Now you can officially join the Single Dad Hockey Players Club. I'm sure they'll help you out. They're pros, after all.

Best, Deidre

Milton Keynes UK
Ingram Content Group UK Ltd.
UKHW051414190624
444445UK00030B/413